# SMALL TOWN FRAME-UP

*A Rolling Brook Novel*

Blye Donovan

*Small Town Frame-up* Copyright © 2022 Blye Donovan

This is a work of fiction. The names, characters, places, and events portrayed in this book are products of the author's imagination or are used fictitiously. Any similarity to real persons, living or dead, or real events is purely coincidental.

No part of this book may be reproduced, or stored in a retrieval system, or transmitted in any form or by any means—electronic, mechanical, photocopying, recording, or otherwise—without express written permission of the author.

Warning: the unauthorized reproduction or distribution of this copyrighted work is illegal. Criminal copyright infringement, including infringement without monetary gain, is investigated by the FBI and is punishable by up to five years in prison and a fine of $250,000.

All rights reserved.

ISBN: 9798986768328
Imprint: Independently published
Cover Design by Central Covers.
Series Logo Design by K.B. Barrett Designs.

# DEDICATION

*This one is for my fellow* Outlander *fans. I hope you fall for Jameson the way I fell for Jamie Fraser.*

# CONTENT WARNING

Contains profanity, mild violence, and mature sexual content.

# PROLOGUE

*Jameson*

Man, it was hot. Why the Rolling Brook Police Department decided to have its annual family barbecue during a heatwave was beyond him. They'd taken over the town park and set up games for the kids, many of whom were screaming their heads off as they walloped each other with water balloons.

While the kids played, the adults were expected to schmooze with the chief's office. Jameson didn't mind schmoozing—usually.

But he'd had enough of it for today.

Watching a feisty little blonde squeal in delight as she beaned a taller boy in the back of the head, Jameson chuckled and thought about joining them merely for the relief of having the cold water burst on his skin—anything to get some relief from the heat.

He remembered coming to this event every summer as a kid. His father had been a police officer until he retired last year. Jameson frowned now, thinking about how happy his mom had been that she and his dad could finally move to Florida. They'd left shortly after that, and his two younger sisters had scattered years earlier.

*I'm the only one left in Rolling Brook.*

The thought caused an ache in his chest. Ignoring it, he took a sip of his beer and cursed—it was already warm.

Despite hiding under the shade of a tall oak tree, sweat dripped down his broad back and added to the discomfort he felt thanks to the basketball injury he'd endured a few days prior.

Which was Dillon's fault, the fucker.

They'd been playing a game of pickup when he went up for a lay-up, and Redland decided to plow into him. He'd landed badly, and his knee had moved the wrong way. It was still sore days later. He hoped it fixed itself soon because he did *not* want to see a doctor for it.

He hated being sick and avoided doctors like the plague, except for the annual physical the department required for all its officers. But if there were a way he could get out of that, too, he would.

Getting grumpier the more he thought about it, Jameson glared across the lawn at his friend. Dillon Redland was standing around with his family and looked completely comfortable in the 92-degree temperature with 80 percent humidity. He, his brother, and his dad all had dark hair and copper skin passed down from their Native American ancestors, though Brock Redland's was streaked with gray.

More sweat trickled between Jameson's shoulder

blades. Sometimes it sucked being a ginger. He wasn't built for this weather. Swiping his hand across his brow, he froze.

*Was that . . . Daisy?* A tall, raven-haired woman ran up to Dillon and hugged him.

*Wow, she looks . . . different.*

She must be back in town, then. He hadn't seen her since she'd left for college. And that had been, what? Ten?

*No. Twelve years ago.*

She'd always been tall, which helped her keep up with him and Dillon growing up, but he remembered her as gangly and not super blessed in the chest department.

The Daisy standing across from him now was neither of those things. She still had those long legs, but they complemented her athletic form. And her chest . . . yeah, those had come in too, and they looked pretty damn impressive in the tight top she was wearing.

*Fuck!*

What was he doing lusting after his best friend's little sister? Even if she was only two minutes younger, that was against the rules—period.

*Sheesh!* He'd even considered her as his own sister when they were growing up.

This was not good.

He cursed himself and was about to turn away when a tall, slick-looking blond sidled up to Daisy. The guy screamed "city" with his expensive shoes and polo shirt. When he put his arm around her waist—a little too low for Jameson's liking—his face turned into a snarl. He was envisioning pummeling the blonde guy into the ground when he stopped himself.

Dammit, he had no right. It had to be the heat making him so crazy.

Unclenching his fists, he turned. His long stride carried him away from their group, quickly across the park to the refreshments table.

What he needed was a damned cold beer and for this obligatory outing to end.

# CHAPTER 1

*18 Months Later*

*Daisy*

Daisy's breath made visible puffs in the air inside the car as she drove to the diner where she worked as lead server. She didn't notice the cold, nor were her thoughts on the music that blasted out of the Honda's tiny speakers. Instead, she thought about the conversation she'd had with her mother the evening before. It was quickly becoming a recurrent one.

Now that her two older brothers were happily paired off, her mom was on her about settling down.

*As if it was that easy.* She rolled her bright blue eyes at no one.

It had been almost a year since she and Derrick broke it off. They'd tried the long-distance thing after she'd moved back to Rolling Brook, but the spark had slowly fizzled out with him in Chicago and her here.

Since the breakup, she'd been on a few dates with a couple of the guys in town, but nothing had made her want to spend longer than that with them. And in the last year, her oldest brother, Jake, had gotten married, and her twin, Dillon, had gotten engaged.

Of course, she was happy for them—ecstatic, really. She loved her current and soon-to-be sisters-in-law, but the more time she spent with all of them, the more she wanted what they had. And she wasn't exactly a spring chicken anymore. Her thirty-third birthday was fast approaching.

Frowning over that fact, Daisy blew through a stop sign. Flashing lights drew her attention, and she glanced in the rearview mirror.

*Oops.*

She pulled to the curb in case other motorists needed to pass, but it was so early that the town felt deserted. It wasn't yet seven in the morning, and Rolling Brook never seemed to stir until closer to eight.

When the police cruiser pulled up behind her, she thought of Dillon and figured at least she had connections if the officer tried to give her a ticket.

She waited until he was right outside her window before she rolled it down, noticing for the first time how cold it was. It was February, and temperatures barely above freezing with a biting wind chill were typical in the Midwest.

"Good morning," she greeted the young officer.

He looked vaguely familiar, but she couldn't quite remember his name. She'd seen nearly everyone in Rolling Brook at some point over the last two years whenever they visited Shug's, the diner where she worked. It was an institution in this town and had been for 74 years. She remembered how much she'd loved coming for the soft-serve ice cream after dinner as a kid, and many Rolling Brook families carried on that tradition.

"Mornin'." A thick strand of light blond hair fell over his forehead as he leaned down and placed his gloved fingers on her window. "You know why I pulled you over, ma'am?"

She almost cringed at the 'ma'am.' He was only being polite, and the term had never bothered her—until recently. She'd missed the point somewhere when she'd transitioned from a "miss" to a "ma'am."

Glum at the thought, Daisy shook it off and answered him. "I am so sorry. I was distracted and ran right through the stop sign."

She used her sweetest smile on him, and when he blushed, his light blue eyes lighting up, she started to feel relieved he wasn't likely to write her a ticket.

But then he cleared his throat and stood abruptly, his cheeks still a little pink. Although, that could just be from the cold. "I'm going to need your license and registration."

Despite the worry settling in her gut, she kept her smile in place. "All right."

She reached over to the glove compartment and dug through the mess inside. Pulling out her registration first, she scrounged through her purse for her wallet and retrieved her driver's license.

Keeping her face pleasant, she handed both of them over. "Here you are, officer."

"I'll be right back. Don't go anywhere."

Sighing as she rolled up her window, Daisy watched the young man climb back into his cruiser. She might need to leverage that familial police connection, after all. However, it would be harder to do at the moment since her brother was in Greece.

He and his fiancé, Lydia, had left recently to visit her family there and take advantage of the warmer weather. Daisy bet it was beautiful this time of year. She'd always wanted to travel but had never made it over the ocean or even past the border.

She *could* always contact James Jameson for help, though she wasn't sure how she felt about asking him to help her get out of a ticket. She would swear the man avoided her on purpose. He never came into Shug's, and he barely spoke two words to her when they happened to run into each other.

It confused the heck out of her. They'd been so close as kids. She'd even had a massive crush on him from the time she'd turned fourteen until she'd gone off to college, though he was too dense to have ever realized it.

She shook her head as she remembered how he and Dillon used to play basketball shirtless on the outside court at the town rec center. As a pretense for staring at Jameson with his shirt off, she'd always offered to referee.

Even as a teenager, he'd been built. And tall, *so* tall. She'd loved that because, at five-ten, she often towered over men. It was nice to find one she had to look up to.

But Jameson had always been dating some blonde or other, and Daisy had never crossed his radar. So, she'd gone to college and forgotten about him—mostly.

The officer knocked on her window and startled her out of her thoughts. She lowered it again, and a blast of cold air hit her.

"Ma'am, I'm afraid I'm going to need to search your vehicle."

"What?" she was surprised enough to blurt out. "Oh, I mean, that's fine. I've got nothing to hide."

He frowned at her. "Step out of the vehicle, please."

She grabbed her gloves from the seat beside her and stepped into the frigid morning air. Pulling the gloves on, she clasped her fingers together while the officer opened her car doors.

He swept his hands under each seat, then went through the center console and the glove compartment. She wasn't sure what he thought he would find, but she knew nothing in her car would get her in trouble.

Drugs or anything of that nature were not what she'd consider a good time, and the most fun she had these days was watching her favorite crime drama before she went to bed.

The officer dug his hands between the seats and came up with a tampon.

*Whoops.* She chuckled at the young man's blush as he put it back where he'd found it.

That might not be the only one he found. Things liked to roll between her seats, and she usually forgot about them. She'd even misplaced a necklace that way, finding it a couple of years later when she'd finally had the car cleaned.

Finished with the interior search, he opened her trunk

and lifted the mat to check underneath it. She thought she had a spare tire under there, but, honestly, she wasn't sure as she'd never needed it.

Apparently satisfied, he closed the trunk and went back around the car, closing all the doors. They'd been open long enough that the interior would be as cold as it was outside, though. She'd been stomping her feet together for the last few minutes in an effort to warm them while he'd searched.

The officer pulled her license and registration out of his pocket and handed them back to her along with a ticket. "Here you are, ma'am. Keep your eyes on the road. You don't want to wind up with a reckless driving charge."

He was still frowning at her, and Daisy wondered why he'd turned so quickly from friendly to stern.

Not wanting to make her situation any worse, she didn't push him. "Yes, I will, officer."

He nodded at her and walked back to his cruiser.

Almost to the point of shivering, she hurried back into her car and cranked the heat up.

That was weird. Why had he needed to search her vehicle? She wished she could call Dillon and ask him, but who knows what time it was in Greece, and she had to get to work. Sighing, she checked the road and pulled back into the non-existent traffic.

When Daisy turned into the parking lot of Shug's, her gaze automatically flew to the metal clock in the center of the restaurant's façade.

*Shoot!*

She was ten minutes late for her shift. Not that Shug would mind. The woman was getting up there in age and often left her to run things, not bothering to come in for the day.

It made her proud that Shug trusted her to manage the diner in her absence. She'd even thought about asking the woman if she could buy her out. Of course, that was a little way down the road. She had to finish her MBA first. The online classes and working full-time were kicking her butt, but she had dreams.

Whether it was Shug's or, one day, a place of her own, she wanted to own a business. She loved feeding people; it was the simplest way to take care of them, and she'd always needed that—to nurture others.

Shug's could be her way of doing that, but she'd have to do some updating first. Not a lot of updating, though; she'd keep the overall squat frame of the building with its bright red paint and rounded corners. They were just too iconic not to.

But the chrome accents could go. Daisy chuckled. The exterior of the building lit up like the fourth of July in summer when the sun shone on it, and you needed sunglasses to keep from being blinded. More than one patron had already complained about it to her.

*Speaking of patrons . . .*

It looked like she already had one.

Mr. Delacourt wouldn't mind, but she didn't want to keep him waiting any longer. Daisy shook herself out of her daydream and scrambled to the diner's matching glass-fronted doors. More chrome gleamed on these, and she grinned, thoughts of exchanging them for wooden ones with pretty oval windows running through her mind. Her brother Jake could make her something like that. He was the best carpenter she knew.

"You're in early for a Sunday, Mr. D.," Daisy said as she entered the diner.

The man was in his seventies but sharp as a tack. She found him seated in his usual spot, all the way at the end of the counter so that he could watch the comings and goings.

"My team's playing at noon. Gotta have lunch at home to catch it."

She chuckled at his enthusiasm. Mr. Delacourt was a big Chicago Bears fan. She was pretty sure the cap he always wore with the football team logo on it was half as old as he was.

"Think you could wrap me up a Reuben to go?" He grinned at her and rubbed his hands together.

Mr. Delacourt ate one of Shug's Reubens at least three times a week. It was a wonder the man stayed as healthy as he did. He wasn't much overweight, and his hat hid a full head of white hair. He'd probably been a redhead at one time because freckles marked his thin, pale skin as much as age spots.

"Of course. Here, I'll pour you some coffee while you wait." She shed her coat and purse, then lifted the flip-up to move behind the counter and get Mr. D. a cup.

Thankfully, Mick had already started the coffee pots for her. The cook must be working on prep because she didn't see him through the window into the kitchen. It wasn't a huge space, and the prep station was the only thing not easily visible through the opening.

After she poured the coffee for Mr. Delacourt, she set it on the counter in front of him. "Here you are. Gimme just a minute while I give Mick your order."

The old man nodded at her. "Sure thing, Daisy. Thank you for the coffee."

She smiled at him before she walked through the swinging door into the kitchen. Mr. D. was her favorite customer. He was a surrogate grandparent of sorts. At least, that's how she thought of him.

Stepping into the small diner kitchen, she found Mick enthusiastically chopping vegetables for the lunchtime stew as he swayed to the music coming out of the tiny radio on the counter above his head. It was Frank Sinatra, and it made her smile.

She loved the classics when it came to music, though she'd hardly recognize anything new since she didn't have time to keep up with it. "Hey, Mick."

"Ahh!" At her greeting, the swarthy, middle-aged cook spun around with a large chef's knife in his hand.

He reminded her of a pirate—a slightly rotund one—with his chestnut hair tied back in a ponytail and his face weathered from his younger days as a professional surfer. All he needed was the eye patch.

"Daisy, never sneak up on a man when he's chopping things."

She chuckled at that. "Sorry if I scared you, but Mr. D. is here, and he wants a Reuben to go."

Mick nodded and laid down the knife. "All right. Have it up in a minute."

"Thanks." She left the kitchen as the man flew into

action. He'd been the head cook at Shug's for nearly twenty years, and she'd bet he could make a Reuben in his sleep.

Back in the main dining room, she called out, "It'll be ready in a minute, Mr. D."

Mr. Delacourt waved a hand, his face buried in the newspaper. He scratched at his forehead and knocked his cap askew. She had the urge to fix it for him, but it had sort of become his signature look.

Instead, she busied herself getting things ready for the customers that would start streaming in after church. She didn't mind working on Sundays, but it was usually their busiest day.

"Order up!" Mick called out through the window and made her jump. He hardly needed to shout when the place was so quiet.

"Thanks for yelling, Mick. I don't know how we would have heard you over the noise out here."

Her sarcasm didn't have the effect she wanted, as Mick had already disappeared. Back to his vegetables, she was sure. She grabbed the sandwich from the window and carried it to Mr. Delacourt.

"Here you are, Mr. D."

"Put it on my tab? I'll settle up on Friday."

She nodded at him. "No problem. Enjoy the game."

At that, he grinned. "Thanks! I intend to. See you tomorrow, Daisy."

"Goodbye, Mr. D." She smiled after him as he collected his newspaper and sandwich and stepped out into the cold.

She shivered when a blast of it blew into the diner and decided to pour herself a cup of coffee to warm up. The quiet part of the morning before the breakfast rush was always her favorite time of the workday. It was the time when she did her planning.

Leaning on the bright white countertop, she gazed around the diner and thought of what she'd change if it were hers. The red stools that lined the counter could stay. She loved that they brightened up the place. The black and white checkerboard on the floor made her dizzy, though. She'd tone that down, maybe with stained concrete or a pattern with red in it that could play off the stools.

The booths lining the wall in front of the counter were old and cracked and would be the first thing she'd replace. They were a muted tan color now, and she thought making them bright red to match the counter stools would bring the place together.

Daydreaming, she stood up and smiled absently as she heard the door open. Her eyes widened when Jameson stepped inside.

He was the last person she'd expected to see.

His cheeks were ruddy from the cold, and his red hair was mussed, giving him a sexy windswept look.

Liking the image, she let her gaze travel across his chiseled jaw and took in the tiny cleft in his chin. When her eyes finally met his light blue ones, she would have sworn she felt a jolt from the intensity he'd leveled at her.

*Well, this day just got interesting.*

# CHAPTER 2

*Jameson*

Daisy stared at him as if he was the last person she'd expected to see. Jameson figured she had a reason to, considering he'd been avoiding her *and* Shug's since she'd started working there. He missed it dearly; his mouth watered every time he thought about one of Shug's Reubens, but it was a self-preservation thing. The less time he spent around her, the less likely he was to do something stupid, like make a move.

As the sister of his best friend—one he'd known since childhood—she was off-limits, out-of-bounds, and completely untouchable.

He hoped it would finally sink in if he told himself enough. So far, his body hadn't gotten the message. Whenever he had to be around her, he felt like a horny teenager.

*But, damn, she looks good.*

His gaze traveled over her. Her dark hair was pulled

back in a high ponytail, exposing her oval face with its prominent cheekbones. Those cheekbones—*mmm*—they were so sexy. He wanted to kiss her there, especially the hollows beneath them. The red diner uniform she wore with its black and white checkered collar fit snugly to her frame, drawing his eyes lower.

He swallowed, realized he was noticeably ogling her, and pulled his eyes back to her face.

Her bright blues were wide as she continued to stare at him. Right, he should probably get this over with.

Clearing his throat, he approached the counter where she stood. "Mornin', Daisy."

"James." Her gaze turned curious as she took him in.

Sighing over the reason he'd come, he pulled the search warrant from the inside pocket of his black police jacket and handed it to her. He started to sweat, but he didn't think it was from the heat inside the diner.

Being confronted with her now after avoiding her as much as he could in a small town, he was nervous as hell.

It had been a shock running into her last summer at Lydia's. And then, with Dillon getting shot and winding up in the hospital, he'd been forced to deliver the news to her. Thankfully, his friend and his new fiancé both came out of that incident alive, but now, months later, his sister was being shoved in Jameson's face again.

After the captain had handed him the warrant this morning, he'd tried to get in touch with her twin but had only succeeded in leaving Dillon a message. Her brother was going to be pissed when he found out.

Jameson wasn't sure who had gone to the county for a

search warrant. He'd tried and failed to get an answer on a Sunday, but a judge had issued a warrant to search Daisy's dwelling. So, here he was, delivering the bad news.

"What's this?" she asked as she accepted the folded papers.

He didn't answer her. She'd find out soon enough.

Daisy unfolded and scanned the documents. "Is this a joke?"

*I wish it were.*

"Come on, James. You got me." She grinned at him. "Did Dillon put you up to this?"

His face was grim when he answered, "It's real, Daisy. I've been ordered to execute it."

Her eyes widened in shock. "What? Why?"

"I need you to come with me." He hated doing this to her, but it *was* his job.

"What's going on? Does this have something to do with the search of my car this morning?"

Her eyes narrowed, and he knew she was struggling to understand how this could be happening to her. Hell, he hadn't figured that out yet, either.

When her words penetrated, he exclaimed, "What? You let someone search your car?" His tone was incredulous. Why the hell would she have allowed that?

She shrugged. "I got pulled over this morning. The young officer said he had to search my car."

"And you let him?" Jameson ran a hand over his face in frustration. "Did he have a warrant?"

"No. At least he didn't show me one. Does that matter?"

"Yes. We can't search without proper authorization.

Unless you allow it, which it sounds like you did. How could you be so—"

"Don't you say it, James," she cut him off, and her eyes snapped at him.

He silently cursed himself. "Compliant. I was going to say 'compliant'."

*Nice save, idiot.*

He could tell Daisy didn't buy it. She glared at him, the blue of her eyes as sharp as steel daggers.

*Fuck.* He was not handling this well.

After taking a deep breath, he started again, "The warrant is for your apartment. Look, the captain sent officers there already. They only have to 'knock-and-announce', but I asked them to wait. I knew you'd be here. The sooner we get over there, the better. I can't promise they'll wait all morning."

She gulped and nodded. "All right. I'll call Shug and be right out."

"Okay." He admired the way the uniform skirt flared over her hips as he watched her walk through the swinging door into the kitchen.

*Focus, James.* Shaking his head at himself, he frowned and turned away to pace.

There was a quiver in his gut, and he didn't like it. Something about this didn't add up. First, her car, now the apartment. What had Daisy gotten herself into?

He didn't have much time to wonder because she was back in under a minute. "That was fast."

She grabbed for her coat and shrugged it on. "Shug is on her way. Since Mick's here, she told me to go ahead."

After picking up her purse, she said, "I'm ready."

"You'll ride with me." He lifted the counter for her and tried not to stare at her ass when she stepped through. Well, he didn't try very hard.

She paused at the door, glancing over her shoulder. "Aren't you coming?"

He was still holding the lift-up counter, staring at her. He let it go, and she visibly winced as it dropped into place with a loud smack.

"Sorry." He shrugged sheepishly. "Right behind ya."

She smirked, and he got the feeling she was onto him.

He felt himself start to blush and let out a string of internal curses. Okay, yeah, maybe he'd wanted to watch her walk away, but if she realized that, he was crossing the line. He needed to keep himself in check, and blushing wasn't helping.

Sure, it was attractive when women blushed, but when a guy did it, it was damned embarrassing. He cursed his fair skin, and the fact that Daisy made him so nervous. It was beyond hard to stay away from her when what he really wanted to do was grab the ass he'd just watched walk away.

He shoved his hands in his pockets and avoided her gaze as he brushed past her out the double doors. "Let's go then."

* * * *

*Daisy*

Daisy's hands alternately clutched and twisted the strap of

her purse as she stared blindly out the cruiser's windshield. Confusion made her thoughts jumbled, and worry had settled into her gut. It was a weight pushing against her stomach the closer they got to her apartment.

*Why on earth would there be a search warrant against me?*

She tried to think of what she must have done for this to be happening. What misstep had she made? Could this all be some horrible mistake? Surely, they'd realize that when they didn't find whatever they were looking for.

*Just like they didn't find anything in my car.*

She shook her head and glanced sidelong at Jameson. His hands were rigid on the wheel, and he stared straight ahead. She was a little perturbed that he'd implied she was stupid.

How was she supposed to know that she could've refused the search of her car? In the crime shows she watched, people agreed or got arrested for not complying.

Sure, that probably wasn't the best source for information, but she'd always been taught to cooperate with the police. And, besides, she didn't have anything to hide.

Confident in that fact, she stopped worrying the strap of her purse and imagined the dressing down she was going to give Jameson when this was all over. Shoot, she may even file a complaint, and the whole dang police department could apologize to her for the invasion of her privacy.

Her face split with a grin. She was imagining him on his knees in front of her, offering her a bouquet of her favorite flower as he apologized when his voice interrupted her fantasy.

"So, this morning? I'm guessing he didn't find anything?"

"Of course not," she scoffed. "Just like you're not going to find anything in my apartment. What is all this about, James?"

"I wish I knew." He glanced sideways at her. "But I'm going to find out. Whatever it is."

Mollified by his response, she decided to let him off the hook . . . for now. "Thank you."

There were two police cruisers already parked outside her apartment when they arrived.

*What do they think they'll find?*

Sighing, she climbed out of the car. She felt like she'd been thrust into one of the crime dramas she enjoyed watching, only instead of starring as the hot-shot detective, she'd become the perp.

Jameson gave a signal to one of the cruisers, and two officers clad in the same black uniform jacket and pants joined them in front of her building.

It was a brick quadplex built in the 1930s. There were a few holes in the exterior where she knew the weather got in, but with paying for her master's degree and trying to save money, it was what she could afford. Thank goodness her neighbors worked during the day and wouldn't be at home.

She didn't savor being the talk of the town, and she'd gladly take any chance she had of keeping this quiet. Glancing around, she didn't see anyone that might gossip.

A few of the buildings on her street were abandoned even. Sadly, several historic ones had fallen into disrepair.

"Let's go, Miss Redland."

Daisy turned, raising an eyebrow at Jameson's formal address. When she didn't move, he gestured at her to unlock the door to the building.

Frowning at the silent officers flanking him, she did as he asked. As she pushed the outer door open, the familiar smell of dust and what she hoped wasn't mold hit her. The entryway was tiny and didn't allow room for all four of them. A wide staircase took up most of the space and led to the two apartments on the second floor. There were two residences on each side of the building with the same footprint on each level. Hers was on the left side of the first floor.

Before she could unlock her door, he stopped her with a hand over hers.

Surprised at the touch, Daisy shot her eyes to his. The warmth from his hand flooded her, and her own started to tingle.

He squeezed her hand, then let go before he addressed the two officers waiting on the doorstep of the building. "I'll go in with her. Follow right behind."

"10-4, sergeant."

She heard the squawk of their two-way radios as they relayed the message to the officers still waiting in the other cruiser, but it was only a buzzing in the background.

Her eyes had locked with Jameson's baby blues again. They were as warm as a summer sky, and she couldn't look away. Her lips parted, and her fingers ached to reach up and brush back the red curls that were falling over his forehead.

His hair was cut short on the sides and the back per department regulations, and she knew the length on top was his way of pushing the limits. She'd always found the rebellious streak in him attractive as a teenager. Apparently, it made her insides fluttery even now.

He cleared his throat and ruined the moment. "Unlock the door, Daisy."

Miffed at his rebuff, she spun around quickly and unlocked her apartment. Chastising herself for losing focus on the reason he was here with her, she stepped inside.

He followed, then moved aside as the two officers pushed past her. She wasn't sure what she was supposed to do, so she hovered by the door.

She wasn't thrilled at the idea of them looking through her things. Was it wrong to follow them? Unsure, she looked to Jameson for guidance.

His expression pinched as he watched the officers begin their search. "I'll stay with her. Let's make this as quick as possible, boys."

They took him at his word.

She gasped when one officer went straight to the kitchen and pulled out all her drawers. As he tossed the contents of each to the floor, the other officer made quick work of her living room. Her apartment had an open-plan concept, and she could see it all, much to her dismay.

They were making a mess of her things.

She propped her hands on her hips as anger began to heat her body. She didn't have much, but she didn't appreciate it being treated so poorly. Boy, was she going to file that complaint when this was over!

Her apartment wasn't large, and they quickly finished the two main rooms. As they disappeared from view to search her bedroom and bathroom, she stared in disbelief at the mess they'd made.

Her living room furniture had been toppled over, and cushions were strewn about the room. Her cookware and utensils littered the kitchen floor. She huffed out a breath and clenched her hands, the nails biting into her palms.

All the while, Jameson stood silently by.

Fighting the urge to yell at him, she turned away. No matter how much that angered her, he was just doing his job.

"What are they looking for?"

"Daisy—" The low tone of his voice drew her gaze, but she didn't get to find out what he was going to say because a shout from the direction of her bedroom called his attention away.

The officers returned to the living room, and one held a package Daisy had never seen before.

"What is that?"

No one answered her. The officer handed the rectangular package to Jameson. It was about the size of his hand, and to her, it looked like it was wrapped in a black garbage bag with mailing tape holding it together.

"What is it, James?"

He looked up from the package, and his eyes speared her. She gulped.

*Uh-oh.*

Whatever it was, it clearly wasn't good. He glanced away, and she exhaled shakily.

"Is this the only one?" He asked the officer who'd brought it to him.

"No, Sarge. There's a stack of at least twenty in the bottom of her closet. Threw a pile of clothes on top like that would stop us from finding them." The officer sneered in her direction, but she was still confused enough not to care.

"What is he talking about? I've never seen that before." Her hands went back to her hips, and she was tempted to tap her foot.

Jameson didn't answer her. Instead, he tilted his head back, eyes looking skyward. "Happy, fucking, Sunday," he growled.

# CHAPTER 3

*Jameson*

"Radio the guys outside and have them come help you carry the rest out," Jameson ordered the rookie in front of him.

The kid was excited about making his first drug bust, but Jameson feared this was much more than a simple drug charge.

When the kid stepped outside and the other officer returned to Daisy's bedroom to guard the stash, he turned to her. "It's drugs. And a lot of them."

"That's ridiculous. I've never done drugs a day in my life." Her hands returned to her hips, and if she weren't about to get hauled into the station, he'd have thought her outrage was cute.

As it was, he simply raised an eyebrow at her.

"Okay, yeah, I tried pot in college, but, come on, whatever that is"—she waved a hand at the plastic-wrapped package they'd found—"it's definitely not mine."

He sighed. "That may be, but it's in your possession."

He knew it wasn't hers in his gut, but she'd gotten herself mixed up in some serious shit.

You didn't wind up with twenty kilos of what he figured was cocaine—though he knew better than to try and get a whiff of it—stashed in your apartment for no reason.

He was going to have to arrest her, and he wasn't looking forward to explaining that to Dillon.

Her mouth fell open at his words. She stood, stunned, and he watched her closely as he asked, "Is there someone else with regular access to your place? A boyfriend or a friend you've given a key to?"

He both hoped and dreaded that she'd have a boyfriend. It could help her case if she did, but despite that, he wanted her to say no. The thought of Daisy with *any* man had his hands clenching into fists.

She frowned at him as if deep in thought. It caused a line to form on her forehead, and he found himself wishing he could smooth it away with his lips.

"My parents have a key, and I gave one to Derrick when I first moved in, but . . . I'm pretty sure he returned it when we split up."

Now, Jameson was the one frowning. "Pretty sure?"

She shrugged at his question.

"'Pretty sure' isn't sure, Daisy. When's the last time you talked to this guy—Derrick?" He almost spat the name. If Derrick had anything to do with what she was currently mixed up in, he'd hunt the fucker down.

She opened her mouth to respond but was interrupted by the rookie returning with the two officers from outside.

"Why haven't you arrested her, Sarge?" His voice was accusatory, but then his brown eyes lit up. "Were you waiting for me?" The young man walked toward Daisy, pulling out his handcuffs as he went.

Jameson put up a hand and stopped him in his tracks. "No. Settle down, Peterson. I'm questioning her."

The rookie frowned at him, and Jameson forced himself to appear bored. "You know this is the lieutenant's sister, right?"

The young rookie gulped, his face blanched, and Jameson tried not to grin. "Still want to be the one to arrest her?"

Peterson shook his head.

"Take this and go help Brooks," he ordered, handing Peterson the package. "I've got her handled."

At his order, the three men retreated to Daisy's bedroom, and he was once again alone with her.

She started to pace, and if not for the situation, it would have made him smile. Her twin did that when he was also trying to work out a problem.

"I asked you a question, Daisy."

"Hmm?" She stopped pacing and faced him, but her eyes told him she wasn't paying attention. Her mind was somewhere else.

"Derrick. When's the last time you had any contact with him?"

"Oh. Um, about a year ago? When we decided to call it off." She flapped her hand like it wasn't a big deal. "It was a mutual thing, and it's not like I expected him to come murder me in my bed. I asked him to mail me the key, and he did—I think."

Jameson ground his teeth together and ran a hand over his face in frustration. "Well, if you're not 100 percent certain, that's something at least."

"Something for what, James? Am I really going to be arrested? You know that stuff's not mine!" Her voice rose on the last statement, and her eyes flooded with tears. She blinked fiercely before turning away from his gaze.

It tore at his insides to see her upset, especially when he knew arresting her was going to make it worse. What he wanted was to pull her into his arms and chase the fear away, but he couldn't—no matter that he believed her.

He sighed heavily before pulling out his handcuffs. Laying his hand on her arm, he turned her to face him.

Her eyes still glistened, but she'd managed to stop the tears from falling. She was biting her lower lip, and for a moment, he stared at it, distracted.

He wanted to put his own teeth there . . . and his tongue. What he wouldn't give to be in her apartment for an entirely different reason . . .

Jameson mentally shook himself out of that line of thinking.

*Fuck, this sucks!*

He needed to help Daisy out of this mess, and itching for her lips on his wouldn't accomplish that.

But, Man, her eyes were killing him. She looked so scared he couldn't help it. He reached up and caressed her cheek. "I'm sorry, Daisy. Truly."

Her eyes filled again, but he turned her around before the tears had a chance to fall.

Lifting his handcuffs, he placed them around her wrists as gently as he could. "Daisy Redland, you're under arrest for the possession of a controlled substance. You have the right to remain silent. Anything you say can and will be used against you in a court of law. You have the right to an attorney. If you cannot afford an attorney, one will be provided for you."

His mouth recited the Miranda warning through habit, but his mind raced as it tried to work out a likely suspect and the motive behind planting drugs in her apartment. "Do you understand the rights I have just read to you?"

When she didn't respond, he moved in front of her. Tears had escaped and tracked down her cheeks.

His gut clenched. "Do you understand?" he asked her softly.

She managed a nod, so he continued, "With these rights in mind, do you wish to speak to me?"

He could read the turmoil in her eyes and wanted to do whatever he could to ease it.

Giving her a slight shake of the head, he mouthed "lawyer," and Daisy understood. "Blair. I'll only speak with Blair."

* * * *

*Daisy*

Daisy was back in the police cruiser with Jameson, but now she sat in the rear with a metal cage separating them. The seats sat higher back there, making the ride cramped and even more uncomfortable. She knew that was the point—to make it harder for an arrestee to attempt anything, but it didn't make her like it any less.

The vinyl was like ice on her bottom; the thin nylons she wore under her uniform afforded no protection from the cold. Her nerves were wound tight, and added to that, the position of her hands cuffed behind her back was causing the muscles in her upper arms to scream. Wishing she could stretch them out, she gritted her teeth and stared out the window.

*Oh no!*

People were going to see her in the back of the police cruiser. That could only be interpreted one way. After this, she was bound to be at the top of the gossip column. As if she didn't have enough to worry about, let's add town pariah to the list. This day was quickly becoming the worst ever, which was truly a bummer considering how it started.

She'd been shocked to see Jameson walk into Shug's this morning, but underneath that had been excitement. The sight of the man sent warmth coursing through her, and with the slightest touch of his hand, he'd caused her breath to quicken and her body to crave more. It had happened even as he'd handcuffed her. Thinking about it now, she felt her face flush.

Seriously, what was wrong with her?

She needed to figure out what was going on, but instead, she'd fixated on Jameson. Daisy rolled her eyes at herself and slunk as far back into the seat as she could, hoping it would make her harder to spot.

They were almost to the station, and the town was much more alive than it had been only an hour before. She started to sweat despite the cold as they drove closer to the tiny white chapel in the middle of town. It was almost time for the Sunday sermon to start, and there were bound to be people in the parking lot next to the church.

*Well, great. Just great.*

Taking a deep breath, she closed her eyes and turned away from the window. She didn't want to know who would see her. Rolling Brook was small, and she would hear about it soon enough.

Tears threatened again, but she refused to let them fall. Who gossiped about her was hardly important right now.

"You okay back there? I don't know that you've ever been this quiet."

At his words, she opened her eyes. Did he actually care, or was he only trying to make her relax? "Yeah, just peachy." She was not in the mood to be pleasant.

"I figured. We'll get to the bottom of this, Daisy. Just hang in there."

His words were meant to be reassuring, but she only felt . . . numb. Her eyelids wanted to droop as though they could shut out this nightmare, and she'd wake to find it had been only that. But she knew she wasn't that lucky. She yawned as they pulled into the parking lot of the police station.

The stucco building had been built in the '50s, and the Art Moderne style had always seemed a little out of place amid the Victorian buildings that lined the street in this part of town.

The station boasted little in the way of decorative features to compete with them. It was rectangular with a flat roof. Unadorned, it looked all business, which, as a cop shop, she supposed it was. But it was business she was currently on the wrong side of.

"We're here." Jameson turned around to face her after putting the car in park. "I'm afraid you're going to hate this next part."

"Oh? Because I've been enjoying myself so much up to this point." She rolled her eyes at the idiocy of his statement.

She heard him sigh before he turned away and climbed out of the cruiser. The door next to her opened, but she wasn't ready to get out. Her stomach was roiling, and she was afraid she might lose the little bit of toast she'd had for breakfast. Hoping she wouldn't embarrass herself further, she closed her eyes and swallowed.

Jameson leaned down and reached for her arm because she'd made no move to get out of the car. "Here, let me help you. It's hard to climb out from the position you're in." She felt his hand close around her upper arm. "Promise not to run?"

She opened her eyes and saw that he was grinning. Her eyes flashed. How could the man be flippant at a time like this?

He must have noticed his teasing hadn't had the desired effect because his grin quickly turned into a frown as he pulled her up and out of the cramped backseat.

"Sorry," Jameson muttered. "Please don't try to knee me in the balls either. I know your M.O., and I'd hate to add 'assaulting a police officer' to your charge sheet."

Oh, she was tempted, just as she'd been many times

before when they were teenagers. Fortunately for him, she'd never succeeded, but it wasn't for lack of trying. She needed him on her side, though, and hurting him wasn't likely to help her.

As the anger left her, the heat from his hand penetrated, and she realized he hadn't let go of her arm. Curious, she looked up at him.

He was staring at her, and the intensity was there again; the light blue of his eyes seemed to pulse. She wished she knew what he was thinking—what made him look at her like that.

After several long seconds, he cleared his throat and turned them toward the entrance. She could either keep up or get dragged as he started for the front steps. It was stupid of her to forget she was in his custody—a suspect, no less. Of course, he wasn't going to let go of her.

Angry with herself, she looked anywhere but at Jameson and was happy to see the street was deserted. At least there weren't more people witnessing her humiliation.

* * * *

*Unknown*

"It's done."

The well-dressed man smiled at the statement. The ring on his hand gleamed when the fluorescent light caught and reflected it where he gripped the telephone.

Swiveling around in his chair, he looked out over the city. It was early morning, and the sun was starting to illuminate the dark corners as it crept in. He preferred the city in the evening when the lights glowed like stars floating in a never-ending sea of buildings. Buildings meant progress, and he hungered for that.

"Excellent. You know what to do next."

"Yes, sir."

The man nodded, though no one else was in the high-rise office to see it. "The woman goes down for this, or you'll take her place."

There was an audible gulp over the line. "Understood, sir."

The man's smile returned. "Good." He hung up the phone and stood, walking to gaze out over the Chicago skyline. His plan was falling into place. Soon, the Redlands would know his wrath.

# CHAPTER 4

*Daisy*

As they stepped inside the police station, the stench of sweat and stale coffee assaulted Daisy's nose. She'd been in the station before and was used to its smell and the noise, but as Jameson escorted her through the bullpen, all eyes turned to her.

Only a handful of officers worked on Sunday, but they all stopped what they were doing at her entrance. It became so quiet she heard her own breaths.

Her face heated with shame, and she cast her eyes downward, staring blindly at the faded laminate tile as they took the final few steps to Dillon's office.

Jameson pulled her through the door and uncuffed her. She was pretty sure that wasn't proper procedure, but she was too happy to be out of handcuffs to care. Her wrists were sore, and she rubbed them as she waited for him to tell her what would happen next.

"Sit down, Daisy. I've got to get you processed." He

moved to sit behind Dillon's desk and scrubbed a hand across his face.

Frowning at his tone, she sat across from him as he booted up the computer. "What does 'processed' mean?"

He didn't look at her as he explained, "It means taking down your personal info, getting your fingerprints, mug shots, and," he paused and gritted his teeth before mumbling, "searching you."

"Okay." She wasn't looking forward to any of that, but at least she wasn't headed for a jail cell . . . yet.

"I'm going to run through the vital information first."

She nodded and waited as he pulled up the forms on the computer.

"Name and date of birth?"

She raised an eyebrow at him and heard his sigh in response. "Just tell me as if I didn't already know the answer."

"Fine. Daisy Sarah Redland. April 8th, 1989."

"Address?"

As she rattled off the rest of the personal information Jameson needed, her mind wandered to how she would get out of this. She needed to call a lawyer, and her sister-in-law Blair was the only one she knew.

But then Jake would find out—and her parents. Daisy cringed. What was her family going to think?

*Cocaine, for goodness' sake!*

She'd never seen the stuff in real life before. When Jameson had told her that's what the drugs were, she'd been stunned.

How in the world had so much of it ended up in her

apartment? It couldn't have been there when she'd left for work. She would've noticed; she was sure of it. Someone had to have gotten in and put it there . . . but *who*? And *how*?

Daisy blinked when Jameson stood. "Time for fingerprints. Let's go."

He took her by the arm as she stood but didn't put the handcuffs back on. Grateful for that, she took a deep breath, and they once again emerged into the bullpen. The room fell silent.

Though her cheeks heated, she held her head up this time and kept pace with Jameson instead of letting him drag her. She was innocent, and she had no reason to let them make her feel guilty. It wasn't her fault she was here, and she was determined to get to the bottom of what was going on.

Her resolve held up as he handed her off to an officer for fingerprinting. It lasted through the horrible mug shot photographs. But it crumpled when he collected her and led her to a small room with a table.

Lying on top was an orange jumpsuit. Staring at it, knowing it meant she'd be staying here longer than she wanted, her heart rate sped, and she became afraid all over again.

Close to panicking, she spun to face Jameson. "I thought I got a phone call!"

He cleared his throat. "You do. After."

She was afraid to ask, but she had to know . . . "After what?"

He rubbed the back of his neck and avoided her eyes.

"After I search you."

*Why won't he look at me?*

Surely, patting her down wouldn't be that bad. It's not like she had anything on her person to hide. "Fine. Just get it over with, please."

She spread her feet and raised her arms, holding them out by her sides. Lowering her lids, she tried not to think about how much she wanted him to run his hands all over her body.

At his cough, she opened her eyes. He was looking at her now, and his face had gone completely red.

*What is he waiting on?*

As he tugged at the collar of his button-up shirt and cleared his throat, it clicked for her.

She dropped her arms, her own face unbearably hot. Her eyes darted to the jumpsuit, and she swallowed.

*No, oh no, no, no.*

"It's a strip search, Daisy."

* * * *

*Jameson*

Jameson was sweating, and he knew his face had to be beet red. He didn't think he could go through with this—job or not.

*But fuck!* The one female officer they had was on vacation, and there was no way he was letting any of those other yahoos touch Daisy. He clenched his teeth at the mere thought of it.

Shuffling on his feet, he noticed her eyes had gone huge

at his statement, so he explained, "It's procedure whenever drugs are involved."

He saw the moment the shock wore off and gave way to anger. Her deep blue eyes narrowed at him. "No, James! You know I'm not hiding drugs." Her hands flew to her hips, and she scowled at him. "Look, I will put on that hideous orange thing if I must, but anything else is just ridiculous."

He wanted to laugh. This whole situation *was* ridiculous. He could believe he was dreaming, except the drugs they'd found in her apartment had been real. She was a suspect, and it was his job to treat her like one, no matter their previous relationship.

*Damn, this sucks.* He ran both hands through his hair and dropped his arms with a sigh. He'd been agonizing over this moment since he'd walked her through the bullpen—knowing it had to be done and that he wouldn't let anyone else do it.

Staring her down, he tried not to admire the fire in her expression. She wasn't a pushover, and he liked that about her. But right now, she wasn't making what he had to do any easier.

As he thought about stripping her of her clothes and touching her in places he'd only fantasized about, his face heated again.

*Dammit!*

He couldn't do this. There was no way he could be detached enough. And he couldn't have her noticing his reaction. His gut told him she wasn't hiding anything, which was a risk he'd have to take.

Sighing in resignation, he turned his back to her. "Just change into the uniform and put your personal belongings on the table."

He heard her soft sigh behind him, and it made his stomach muscles tense. What he wouldn't give to hear her sigh in satisfaction like that after he'd made her—*Fuck! Think about something else.*

The sound of buttons being undone and clothes sliding to the floor was exquisite torture. She was naked behind him, and what he wanted more than anything was to turn around and see her. But . . . he had a damn good imagination.

Realizing he was grinning, he mentally slapped himself. *Get it together, asshole, before she notices your raging hard-on.*

"Okay, I'm changed." Her voice was flat and held none of the heat she'd tossed at him only moments before.

He silently cursed and adjusted himself before turning back around. Damn, she was sexy. The orange jumpsuit should have been unflattering, but she'd cinched the waist so that it showed off her subtle curves. With her long legs, the uniform actually fit. There was no bunched material at the bottom; the color even complimented her skin tone and dark hair. But her blue eyes were no longer bright, as though putting on that uniform had dulled her fire. The realization cooled his libido and sent a pang arrowing through his chest.

"What now?" Her eyes glistened with unshed tears, and it took every ounce of willpower he had not to pull her into his arms and comfort her.

Jameson shook himself and cleared his throat. "I'll, um, get this stuff handed off, and you can make that phone call."

* * * *

*Daisy*

Three hours. That's how long Daisy had been sitting in the small eight-by-nine holding cell. A clock hung across the room, and she'd watched through the metal bars that made up the entry wall as its hands moved around it. The ticking was her only companion. Her accommodation was bare, apart from a toilet in one corner and the metal bench she perched on lining the far wall. The cinder block construction made the room cold, and the air stank of the cell's previous occupants. Her one measure of gratitude was that she was the only inhabitant. She didn't want to think about sharing the small space with someone else.

Sighing, she leaned her head back against the wall and closed her eyes. The movement sent the musty smell of the uniform she'd been forced to wear wafting into her nostrils. Someone must have folded the fabric and put it away before it was completely dry. She hated that smell and wanted to put back on her clothes more than anything.

Thinking about being forced to change into the orange jumpsuit brought with it the image of Jameson, red in the face and downright uncomfortable, telling her he had to strip search her. The indignity of it made her cringe, but really, would it have been so bad? The way he'd acted, you would've thought she was a leper. The man was beyond frustrating. He could be so kind one minute, like when he'd caressed her cheek before he'd handcuffed her, yet so disparaging the next.

Daisy lifted her hand and pressed it to the spot where she could still feel his touch. His gentleness had surprised her. He'd been distant since she'd moved back, but to touch her like that . . . he had to care. Didn't he?

They'd been close when they were younger—her, Dillon, and Jameson. But perhaps that was the problem. Did he see her as only a sister? Did his kindness toward her stem from that?

In disgust at herself, she let out a strangled noise and dropped her hand. *Ugh!* She was doing it again.

There were so many other things she needed to think about, yet here she was pining over Jameson. He clearly wasn't interested in her that way. If she hadn't gotten arrested, they wouldn't be spending time together now.

*Arrested.* Daisy shook her head.

This whole day had been surreal. She was sitting in a jail cell, but the fact that she'd been incarcerated still hadn't fully sunk in. That sort of thing only happened in the crime shows she watched, not in real life. Except . . . she'd been given her phone call and had talked to Blair.

Now, her family knew she was here. They'd go to her arraignment, which she hoped would happen soon. Spending the night in this cell was at the top of the list of things she never wanted to do. A shiver ran through her as she thought about that possibility.

Blair had advised an overnight stay was likely on a Sunday. Since she'd been a criminal defense attorney in

Chicago before moving to Rolling Brook, Daisy trusted her opinion. Her head had wanted to spin when Blair started to explain how things would work. It all sounded way more complicated than what they showed you on television.

There was the arraignment and a possible bail hearing before she'd be released. On top of that, it was public, which meant anyone could watch her humiliation. She was happy it meant her family would be there to support her, but the thought of anyone else watching made her stomach knot. There was no chance the whole town wouldn't know about this by tomorrow. She was going to be the butt of gossip for sure.

Groaning, she sat up straighter and opened her eyes. She gasped in surprise to find Jameson watching her outside her cell.

His gaze was penetrating, and she wished—again—that she knew what he was thinking. She stared back, searching, then he blinked, and the intensity disappeared.

He avoided her eyes as he approached the door to her cell and placed the key in the lock. "It's time, Daisy."

# CHAPTER 5

*Jameson*

Daisy didn't look relieved at his announcement. She had to be scared, but at least she was getting out of this cell. Jameson had been working hard over the last three hours to make sure she didn't spend the night in there. He'd tried to get ahold of her brother again, only to leave Dillon another voicemail.

After finishing his report, he'd hand-delivered it to the district attorney's office, intent on forcing the charges to be drawn today. Of course, the DA wasn't in the office on a Sunday, but Jameson had turned on the charm and convinced the young law clerk on duty to do him a favor.

Ever since the show *Outlander* became popular, convincing women to do all manner of things for him was not a problem.

At first, he'd enjoyed the comparison to the series' tall, red-headed Scot—Jamie Fraser—and the amount of action it got him. But now, at thirty-three, Jameson was tired of women who only wanted to fulfill a fantasy. He wasn't a fictional character, and none of those women he'd been with had cared to get to know the real James Jameson.

He might be a tall redhead of Scottish descent, but he was firmly rooted in the here and now—not eighteenth-century Scotland or whenever that show was set.

Layla, the blonde who'd practically shoved her generous assets in his face, had contacted the district attorney at his home and started the arraignment ball rolling. She'd been gracious enough to provide Jameson with her phone number, too.

Not that he planned on doing anything with it. He'd tossed it in the can outside the building. There was only one woman he was interested in, and right now, she needed his help.

He pushed open the door to Daisy's cell. She'd stood when he'd unlocked it but hadn't moved to exit.

Because her eyes stared through him, he smiled and teased her, "I thought you'd be happy to be leaving this place."

At that, her gaze shifted to his, and their spark returned. "I am! The less time I have to spend in jail, the better." The fire quickly left her, and she hugged her arms over her chest. "But, what now? I feel . . . helpless, not knowing how to get out of this mess."

She stared up at him, her gaze imploring as she nibbled at her bottom lip.

A part of him wanted to pull her into his arms and soothe her fears away. His eyes narrowed as he watched her teeth assault the supple skin of her lips. Their plum color deepened, and he couldn't help imagining what they'd feel like wrapped around his—

"James?"

He blinked and cleared his throat, avoiding her gaze as color flooded his skin. He stepped to the side and motioned for her to step forward. Before she'd made it through the cell door, he cursed, remembering he had to restrain her again.

"Wait, Daisy." Sighing, he pulled his handcuffs from his belt. "I have to cuff you."

She froze, and her shoulders drooped at the news. Then she reached her arms behind her back.

He frowned and turned her to face him. "No." He moved her arms, placing them together in front of her, and gestured for her to hold them up, wrists facing each other. "This way is fine."

"Thank you." It was barely a whisper from her lips, and he fought the urge to hold her.

Knowing he shouldn't, he settled for gently squeezing her arm in reassurance before turning her toward the exit. "After you."

* * * *

*Daisy*

Not ready to leave the anonymity of the cruiser, Daisy stared up at the Dale County courthouse. The building had probably been beautiful once. The brick that made up its two stories had started as a light pink color, and the stone that served as an architectural feature was white at one time—but years of dirt had washed out the color of the bricks while pollution had stained the stone. Even the central dome that rose an extra story above the building's flat roof showed signs of damage. Rust stains dripped from the metal siding, adding to the general air of negligence.

In the waning light of a winter afternoon, the courthouse seemed only to offer despair. She hoped her predicament wouldn't end in such a state.

Taking a deep breath to calm her nerves, she steeled herself as Jameson opened her door. He offered his hand, and she grasped it with her cuffed ones.

*Might as well get this over with.*

The cold air helped clear her head as he walked her to the building. The parking lot was nearly empty, and no one bustled about. She thought maybe she'd be lucky with the lack of activity, and no one from town would have come to watch her arraignment. She could use any favors right now—small or large. The only person she wanted here was her lawyer, and Blair should be waiting for her inside.

His hand was warm on her arm through the horrid orange jumpsuit she still wore. She tried not to let his touch affect her, knowing she had more important things to think about, but it was as if a current connected them. Every time he touched her, she felt its zap.

As they stepped inside the central rotunda, her spirits lifted slightly at the beauty of the interior. This part of the building had been immaculately preserved. She gazed up through the dome and admired the way the light bounced off the coffers that decorated its ceiling. The pink from the exterior brick echoed in the decorative trim and architectural molding. Lost in admiring it, she felt a slight shake of her arm.

"Hmm?" Her head snapped back down to find Jameson frowning at her.

"I said, 'The courtroom is through this door.'" He dropped her arm and pointed.

Her chest tightened with the reality of her situation intruding. "For my arraignment." Her voice came out in a monotone as she stared at the ornate wooden door he indicated.

"Yes . . ." he hesitated. His forehead wrinkled as he rubbed at his jaw.

She glanced at him and noted the indecision on his face. "What is it, James?"

"You talked to Blair? You know what to expect?" He ran his hand through his hair, and her eyes followed the movement, her own hands itching to do the same.

Shaking herself, she met his gaze. "Yes. They'll read the charges and ask how I plead. I'm surprised they got it scheduled so soon. Blair said it'd probably be tomorrow at the earliest."

When he blushed and looked away, she said, "You did this, didn't you?"

At his shrug, she smiled, happy he'd kept her from spending the night in jail. Leaning in, she kissed the cheek he'd turned away from her. "Thank you."

She'd only meant to give him a quick peck but leaned in too far. With her bound arms caught between them, she managed to lose her balance.

His arms came up reflexively to steady her as she

crashed into his broad chest. Hard muscles broke her fall. The man was solid as a rock.

She inhaled a sharp breath at the sensation of him pressed full length against her. The scents of coffee and something oaky that she thought must be his aftershave filled her nose. It was all male and suited him.

When he cursed, she mumbled an apology, trying to right herself by pushing off his incredibly hard abs.

Before she could manage it, he jerked her upright. Then he dropped his hands from her arms as though she'd scalded him and stepped away from her.

*Great job, Daisy. Make the man who's helping you even more uncomfortable.*

"James, I didn't mean—"

"No more stalling. It's time to go in." He wouldn't look at her.

She sighed when he opened the courtroom door. Well, the arraignment couldn't be any more embarrassing than that.

* * * *

*Unknown*

The golfer's hand tightened around the putter as he thought about the news he'd just received. They'd let the Redland woman out on bond. It wasn't what he'd wanted, but the man who failed him in that regard wouldn't do so again. In fact, it only made his plans for her future more certain.

His fingers relaxed as he acknowledged the advantage

he now had to play. Flexing them, he grinned down at the ring on his right hand. She would be found guilty no matter her plea. That was the advantage of having . . . *certain* connections. They'd already proven themselves by getting the charges brought against him dropped.

He was a man who wouldn't let that kind of afront go unpunished. That's why her farmer brother and that whole dastardly family would pay.

Confident in the knowledge, the golfer sent the ball home with one stroke.

*Ace.* He smiled, blue eyes glinting in satisfaction.

With the flick of his hand, an assistant scrambled to retrieve the ball from the indoor putting green.

The golfer handed the young man his putter and patted his blonde hair back in place. "That'll be all for tonight."

"Yes, sir." The young man didn't need to be told twice. He quickly disappeared.

The golfer knew his employees were a little bit afraid of him. He liked it that way. Fear bent people to your will just like it would bend the judge he was going to pay a visit to. Because it was time he got what he was owed from the Redlands.

# CHAPTER 6

*Daisy*

Daisy stared out the car window as Blair drove her home. Snow-coated trees passed by in a blur, but what she saw was the courtroom where her life had turned upside down. She could still hear Judge Clovis's decision ringing in her head.

*Daisy Redland, the defendant, is hereby charged with the illegal possession of cocaine with intent to distribute. You are being released on an unsecured bond until the date of your trial. Your release is in effect under the following conditions: you are not permitted to use drugs or alcohol, to associate with known criminals, to possess weapons, or to travel outside this state. If the defendant violates any of these conditions, this court will hold you in jail without option for release until the date of your trial. Is that clear?*

It was clear, all right. The formal proclamation had chilled her to the core. She'd been lucky the judge was a regular at Shug's, or she wouldn't have gotten off so easily.

Not that facing criminal charges was easy, but at least she hadn't had to post bail upfront. Every dime she had in savings was for her future business, and she didn't want to waste it on a crime she didn't commit.

She sighed and leaned her head back against the seat, closing her eyes. The whole thing had happened so fast. At least Blair had been brilliant. A small smile moved Daisy's lips as she recalled how fierce her sister-in-law had appeared despite her petite stature.

With her long blonde hair secured in an elaborate chignon and her green eyes shrewd as a snake, Blair had been the picture of confidence as she'd argued for Daisy's case to be dropped.

But all those packages of cocaine had been too damning. She inwardly cringed as she recalled the look on her parents' faces when the DA had read the charges against her. They'd been shocked, and she knew the feeling. She still didn't understand how the drugs had gotten into her apartment, but she was determined to find out—with or without Jameson's help.

The man hadn't looked at her once during the arraignment, nor had he said more than two words to her afterward. Had that simple kiss on the cheek crossed a line?

She'd only wanted to convey her gratitude that he'd sped up the arraignment. But maybe he'd thought she was coming on to him. She hadn't meant to literally fall all over him.

*It had been an accident, darn it! Agh! This has to be the worst day ever!*

"We're here." Blair's soft voice broke into Daisy's thoughts.

She opened her eyes to see they'd parked in front of her apartment.

Blair reached across the seat and placed her hand on Daisy's arm. "Do you want me to come in with you?"

She blinked and turned to face her sister-in-law. "No." She placed her hand on Blair's and said, "Thank you, but I just want to go to bed. Today has been the longest day, and I have to get up early for work tomorrow." Truthfully, Daisy was bone-tired, but she wasn't sure she'd be able to sleep.

Blair squeezed her arm, then let go. "I understand. If you need to talk or have questions, just call. I'll check on you tomorrow, okay?"

She nodded, then grabbed Blair in a fierce hug. "Thank you for all your help." She swallowed back the sob that wanted to rise up her throat. "I'm lucky to have you as my lawyer."

Blair patted her on the back. "We'll get through this, Daisy. Don't worry."

Feeling the tears that threatened, she took a deep breath and released her sister-in-law. "Thank you."

Turning away quickly, she climbed out of the car and waved. She wanted to get inside before she lost control. There were so many emotions swirling around in her gut—embarrassment, shame, fear, worry—that she wasn't sure if she'd cry, vomit, or pass out.

She struggled to place the right key in her lock with teary eyes. When she finally succeeded, she let out a cry of despair at the state of her apartment. The tears flowed freely down her cheeks as she took in the toppled furniture.

Somehow, in all that had happened today, she'd forgotten about the disarray her apartment had been left in, but no matter where she looked, she couldn't escape the stark reminder of the mess her life had become.

After several seconds, she shook herself and wiped angrily at her tears. Crying wasn't going to clean anything. She shrugged out of her coat and purposefully hung it in her hall closet. Next, she set to re-righting her living room and kitchen. She focused solely on putting items back where they belonged and didn't let her mind stray to things she no longer had the energy to think about.

Once she'd finished putting her apartment back together, she glanced at the clock on her microwave. It was nearly eleven, and she had to be up at six. Groaning, she dragged herself to the bathroom for a hot shower. After letting the water work on the tension in her back, she climbed into bed. Though she'd tried to avoid them, thoughts of Jameson crept in.

He'd said he'd help her get to the bottom of this, but she worried he'd changed his mind after her embarrassing stumble. Or because of the kiss. It hadn't even been a real kiss. Still, she remembered how his stubble had felt against her lips and how that current had made her nerve endings buzz everywhere their bodies connected.

*What would it be like to kiss him for real?* To have him crush her against him instead of shoving her away.

*And his body, mmm . . .*

He'd been impressive as a teenager, but the muscles

she'd felt today had been a surprise. She wanted to see what all that hardness looked like.

*No use fantasizing about it now.*

After his reaction today, she wasn't sure she'd ever get the chance. But what she did know was she needed his help. She had no idea how to go about tracking down whoever had put those drugs in her apartment, but *he* had to have a way.

* * * *

*Jameson*

Sweat soaked Jameson's hair and made his red curls mat to his forehead as he swung with a lead hook into the black punching bag that hung in the corner of his living room. An upbeat tune played softly out of the Bluetooth speaker that perched on a shelf behind the bag. He'd have blasted the music if it wasn't nearly midnight and his landlady didn't live next door. She was probably asleep, and he didn't need her showing up, thinking he'd meant to wake her as an invitation—again.

Yeah, he swiped at the sweat on his forehead before it could drip into his eyes. He learned that lesson the hard way.

In any case, he needed to box. It aided his thinking and also helped him work off . . . frustration. And boy, did he have a lot of that where Daisy was concerned.

*Like a never-ending case of blue balls.*

He grimaced and hit the bag with a series of punches— jab, cross, rear hook, uppercut. Breathing heavily, he grabbed it to stop the swinging, which caused the excess chain to bang into itself.

Why was he so attracted to Daisy? She wasn't even his usual type. He executed a feint, then swung at the bag with another lead hook.

Blonde and busty had always been his thing. Daisy was neither of those. Maybe it was the fact she was off-limits that made her so enticing. He'd always had a rebellious nature, courtesy of growing up with a cop as a father. He still wasn't sure how he ended up one himself. It suited him most days. But not when he was arresting the sister of his best friend, and, oh yeah, he had the fucking hots for her.

*Dammit! What a shitty day.*

His face turned into a snarl, and he went at the bag again—jab, jab, cross, lead uppercut.

What did she mean kissing him like that? He had enough trouble trying to keep his hands off her, and she goes and falls into his arms. Some cruel joke from the universe, probably.

Unless . . . had she meant to do it? Plenty of the women he'd been with had no qualms about openly flirting with him and a few of them had used those kinds of tactics. But would Daisy? Or did he only wish that she had?

Grimacing at his stupidity, Jameson let loose and swung at the bag. This time, his blows landed with enough vehemence to send it banging into the wall.

*Fuck!* He quickly stilled the heavy bag and strained to hear any movement next door. Right now, he really didn't want to have to deal with a scantily clad, sleep-mussed

Shelly.

After several long seconds, he let the punching bag go along with the breath he hadn't realized he was holding. All remained quiet.

Shaking his head at himself, he undid the straps on his boxing gloves and tossed them to the floor. Swiping at the sweat on his forehead with a forearm, he moved to the kitchen for a glass of water.

As he filled a cup from the tap, he acknowledged Daisy would never do that. She had meant the kiss as a thank you—nothing more. And why was he obsessing over it anyway? Probably because he couldn't get the feel of her perky breasts and taut body out of his head.

After a frustrated sigh, Jameson downed the water in one gulp and grabbed a towel from the counter to wipe his face. What he needed to focus on was who was framing her. Not whether she'd been flirting with him.

He tossed the towel aside and leaned back against the kitchen sink. That's absolutely *not* the information her brother was going to want.

Frowning, he massaged the back of his neck. Getting ahold of Dillon was a top priority. His fiancé, Lydia, had mentioned they'd planned on sailing, but it was the twenty-first century. How did they not have access to a phone?

Jameson scowled. He'd keep trying. And if he didn't get through, surely Dillon's family would.

Scrubbing a hand across his chin, he replayed the day's events. Someone had issued the search warrant. Finding out what had led to that was where he would start while the county narcotics unit focused on the drugs.

Resolved in his plan, he nodded to himself and pushed off the sink, needing a shower and sleep.

If the arraignment was any indication, Daisy was in good hands with Blair *if* her case went to trial.

Still, he hoped it wouldn't get to that point. He knew she was innocent; now he had to figure out how to prove it.

# CHAPTER 7

*Daisy*

"Daisy?"

"Hmm?" She'd been absently staring at the clock behind the counter for the last ten minutes. Time was dragging, but she only had five minutes left on her shift.

Five minutes until she could escape—away from the watchful eyes and hushed whispers of the diner customers.

She started when Mr. Delacourt placed his hand on her arm. He withdrew it quickly but pressed, "Are you all right, girl? I know they've been tough on you today, but this'll blow over, and they'll be after the next piece of gossip tomorrow."

At his reassurance, Daisy smiled, though it didn't quite reach her eyes. "Thanks, Mr. D. I hope you're right."

She grabbed a washcloth and started to wipe the counter down. Anything to make these last—she glanced back at the clock—four minutes and twenty seconds go by quicker.

The door opened, and she couldn't contain the sigh that escaped.

*Great. More customers wanting to see 'the criminal.'*

She didn't bother looking up. Her relief was due here any minute; Amber could deal with this customer.

But as usual, Amber was running late. Daisy was scrubbing furiously at a stain on the counter when a large hand stilled hers. She sucked in a breath and glanced up to find Jameson frowning down at her.

"Are you off shift soon? We need to talk."

Surprised to see him, she managed a nod. His cheeks were red from the cold, but the smudges under his eyes told her she wasn't the only one who had a restless night.

He was still touching her, and the warmth from his hand spread through her. Her thoughts were vying against the sensation, which, added to the stress of the day, made her feel like a distracted mess.

He raised an eyebrow at her, and she blinked.

*Why is that so sexy?*

Her thoughts ran in a direction she didn't want them to go. He was waiting for something, wasn't he?

Pulling herself together, she straightened off the counter and shook her head. "No, I mean. I can't. Not until Amber gets here."

There was a tightness in his features that had her wondering what he wanted to talk to her about. Finally, he released her hand, and she let out a small breath of relief. Things would be a lot easier if he'd stop touching her like that.

"No problem. I'll wait." He sat on the stool beside Mr.

Delacourt and stared at her.

"Ah, did you want a coffee or something?" She had never been tongue-tied by a man before, but she found herself floundering with Jameson.

*Must be the stress of today . . . or the lack of sleep.*

"Sure, thanks." He blinked, and she looked away. The man's eyes had some strange power over her. Whenever he held her gaze, she couldn't seem to break it.

Released from his baby blues, she busied herself making a fresh pot of coffee, cursing Amber, who was now three minutes late the entire time.

Mr. Delacourt had watched the exchange between Daisy and Jameson with unabashed interest. A knowing smile lit his face, and he chuckled into his coffee mug.

As soon as she set a cup of the fresh brew in front of Jameson, his phone rang. He stood and pulled it out of the pocket of his jeans—jeans that strained over muscular thighs. Daisy gulped and brought her eyes back up.

*Stop ogling him! What is wrong with you today?*

"I'm sorry. I have to take this." He stepped outside in two quick strides to answer the call.

She was staring after him until she felt a tap on her shoulder.

Amber shed her coat and said, "Sorry I'm late! With this cold weather, my car didn't want to start."

"Oh, that's okay. Thanks, Amber." Daisy turned her attention back to Jameson.

She could see him clearly through the diner windows as he talked and paced. He seemed agitated, and she wondered what the phone call was about.

Amber peered around her shoulder. She was several inches shorter than Daisy, blonde, and about as nosy as it gets. "Is that Officer Jameson? Oh! I hope he comes in here. He used to come in all the time, but I haven't seen him in forever. Isn't he yummy! Those broad shoulders and all that red hair. Mmm, I could just—"

"Amber!" Daisy admonished. The woman had no shame and paid no attention to the fact that half the diner could hear her.

The blonde laughed and shrugged. "Well, he is. Have you seen *Outlander*? He's like a real-life Jamie Fraser. Who would pass that up?"

With that, Daisy had had enough. She grabbed the smaller woman's arm and dragged her into the kitchen. Mick glanced up at them but returned to the stove at her sharp head shake, promptly ignoring them.

She dropped Amber's arm, and her hands instinctively went to her hips. "No. I don't know what *Outlander* is. But that's beside the point. If you want to ogle men, do it on your off time."

She took a deep breath while the blonde stared at her in shock. "Now, I can forgive you for being a few minutes late for car trouble, but once you're on the clock, you're on the clock, got it?"

She'd never been so stern with an employee before and knew she was letting the stressful day get to her.

Amber seemed to recover because her face broke into a grin. "You like him!"

"What? Did you hear any of what I just said?" Daisy tapped her foot in frustration.

"Yes, and you have it bad, sister. I know a jealous woman when I see one." The blonde bimbo had the audacity to wink at her.

Daisy was sure steam was about to come out of her ears.

Shug's arrival saved her from saying something she was likely to regret. "Now, what's all this? I've got customers asking for service out front, and you two are back here bickering like old hens."

The older woman's voice was gravelly, courtesy of too many years as a heavy smoker, and the sound of it sent a shot of dread through Daisy's bones. She hadn't heard her boss come in.

*Great. Way to show Shug you can handle the place.*

"Amber, girl. Why are you still here? Get out there and take care of the customers." Shug was a good six inches shorter than Daisy, but what her boss lacked in height, she more than made up for it in spunk.

The blonde blinked at Shug's order and sprang into action. "Yes, ma'am!"

When she disappeared through the swinging door, Daisy sighed. She'd have to deal with Amber eventually. For now, she just wanted to go home.

"I'm sorry, Shug. She was being inappropriate and—"

"I'm sure you had a good reason to pull her in here. That girl's mouth tends to run away with her. What I want to know is, are you all right?" Shug's wrinkled face was full of concern as she waited for an answer.

Daisy tried to nod in response, but she knew her expression had given her away. When the woman's plump arms came around her in a hug, she had to blink back the tears.

Shug rubbed Daisy's back as she held her. "You'll get through this. Anyone with sense knows you're innocent." Pulling back, she held Daisy at arm's length as she gave her a once-over with a pair of shrewd light brown eyes. Inspection complete, the older woman nodded her head. "Why don't you take a couple days off. You've been working too hard for too long."

Days off sounded like heaven, especially if it meant she didn't have to face the gossipmongers. But she couldn't leave Shug shorthanded. "Are you sure? I don't want to leave you in a lurch."

"Don't you worry about it. I haven't spent enough time here lately. A couple days of real work, and maybe I'll be ready to retire." Shug winked at her, and Daisy let out a weak chuckle.

"Thank you. I hate to admit I need it." She squeezed the older woman's hands in gratitude.

"Everybody needs help sometimes. The strong ones don't like to ask for it." She snatched up Daisy's coat and purse and shoved them at her. "Now, scoot. I don't want to see you back here before Monday."

Daisy smiled and headed for the back exit, not wanting to run into Amber or any of the diner patrons. She'd had all the questions she could take for one day.

Trying to put her coat on while holding her purse and walking was not an easy task. She'd almost accomplished it when she reached the exit. Because she wanted desperately to get out of there, she was moving to push on the back door with her hip when it flew open.

Not expecting that, she toppled into Jameson. Her momentum carried them forward—or backward, in his case—causing his foot to slip on the icy steps. That sent them both tumbling to the ground in an awkward heap. Daisy's purse went flying, and the phone Jameson had been holding hit the pavement with a crunch.

"Ow!" she yelped when her right knee connected with something sharp.

"Dammit!" Jameson growled as his head smacked the ground with a thud.

Having landed mostly on top of him, Daisy was the first to recover. She wiggled, trying to push herself upright. One arm hadn't made it entirely through the coat sleeve, and it was currently trapped between her and Jameson.

"Stop moving," he warned through gritted teeth.

"Sorry, but I'm stuck. You're on top of my coat." She pushed herself up as much as she could and tugged at the sleeve, but it didn't budge.

The man might as well have been a boulder. Resigned that the only way she was getting her coat back was for him to get up, she lay still and waited, savoring the contact.

Her flesh pebbled, but she didn't feel the cold. With her face pressed into his chest, Jameson's woodsy scent washed over her, and she closed her eyes, imagining his arms had come around her and that they were locked in a very different type of embrace.

*If only.*

Several seconds passed, and he hadn't moved. As much as she was enjoying this, she was beginning to worry about him.

"Are you all right, James? We should get up before someone sees and wonders what's going on."

*And* more *gossip starts.*

He growled something unintelligible but lifted his back enough that she could pull her coat out from underneath him. "Thank you."

She sat up and finished putting on her coat, focusing on anything but the gorgeous man lying next to her.

"I think you cracked my skull," he grumbled.

"I doubt it," she absently answered as she examined the tear in her hose and the nasty scrape on her knee. It was going to need to be cleaned out and bandaged. The nylons were toast, but the rest of her was unscathed.

"Fuck!"

Surprised at the expletive, Daisy glanced over at Jameson to find him sitting up and clutching his head.

"What's wrong?" Instinctively, she reached for his head and started patting. When her hand connected with the back of his skull, she gasped.

"Argh! Daisy, be careful."

She stared down at the blood that covered her hand and gulped. "James, you're bleeding."

"Yeah, I noticed." He stopped clutching his head and looked at her. "Have you always been this klutzy?"

"Me! This was *your* fault. What were you doing coming through the back door anyway?" Her breathing was heavy from a bewildering mixture of desire and anger as she glared at him.

When he shifted, she caught his grimace of pain.

Shaking her head, she got herself under control. "You know what? It doesn't matter. Let me look at your head."

"It's fine," he snarled at her as he slowly stood up.

Frowning, she watched him closely as she gathered her purse and the spilled contents. He reached back to check the wound and blanched when he made contact.

Yep, she was taking a look at that whether he wanted her to or not.

Determined to railroad him if need be, she slung her purse on her shoulder as he bent down to pick up his phone. When he stumbled and almost fell, she rushed to his side.

"You're not fine!" She moved quickly and secured Jameson's arm over her shoulders. Holding onto his side with her other arm, she hoped they didn't topple under his weight.

She wasn't a small woman at five feet, ten inches, but the man had to have a good fifty pounds on her.

*Or more.* She thought, remembering muscle was heavier than fat. And he was all muscle; at least, that's what it had felt like to her when she'd been lying on top of him.

He groaned. "Just help me sit down for a minute."

As she lowered them onto the steps they'd recently fallen from, her thoughts raced in a worried frenzy. What if he had a concussion? Should she call an ambulance? Did she break the one man who could help her?

*Darnit! This is just my luck.*

* * * *

*Jameson*

Did the woman ever stop talking? As Daisy fretted over him, Jameson closed his eyes and focused on breathing through the pounding in his skull. If he'd thought yesterday had been rough, today now topped it.

He'd spent all day wading through red tape to find out who had issued the search warrant against Daisy. As soon as he had, alarm bells had gone off.

As far as he could tell, the warrant had originated with a judge who tended to let criminals off easy if it meant ruling in favor of progress. Not only that but where was the probable cause? How had the judge known there'd be evidence of a crime in her apartment?

Of course, as soon as Jameson brought this up to the captain, the man shot him down. According to his superior, he had no business looking into the warrant to begin with. What did it matter who had issued it?

A great deal, he believed. He planned to pay the judge a visit, regardless of what the captain said. Jameson's hands clenched into fists as he thought about it.

He'd struck out again with Dillon, and he could really use the lieutenant's help with this. Dillon would have his back against the captain no matter what. But he wasn't here, and Jameson couldn't wait. Daisy needed him.

Fucking, Daisy. How she'd managed to knock him flat on his ass like that, he wasn't sure. The woman was a force to be reckoned with.

As soon as he'd finished his call, he saw that the blonde server had relieved Daisy. Not wanting a run-in with the persistent Amber, he'd gone around back expecting to catch Daisy there. And he'd caught her all right.

As if cracking his head on the pavement wasn't bad enough, then he'd had to deal with her sprawled all over him. Okay, maybe he'd enjoyed that part. Maybe he'd lain there a little longer than he'd needed to. But it was torture, all the same, knowing he couldn't take it anywhere. The head injury had to be payback.

He opened his eyes and grimaced at the sky. The universe was making him suffer for lusting after his best friend's sister. That or Daisy was trying to kill him. At the moment, it felt like she'd made a damn good pass at it.

He sighed and stared at the empty street. At least his vision wasn't blurred.

She was still talking, but he started paying attention at the word 'hospital'.

"I'm not going to the hospital!" He broke out in a sweat at the mere mention of it. He didn't do doctors, and he absolutely didn't do hospitals. Hospitals were for severe injuries, things you couldn't fix on your own, like a gunshot wound—not a bump on the head.

"James, I think you should get checked out. What if you have a concussion?" Her voice quivered with worry, but he wasn't giving in.

"Then there's nothing they can do for me anyway." He glared at her to get his point across.

"Why are you so stubborn?" She huffed in exasperation. "At least let me look at your head."

If he weren't pissed at her for breaking his head open in the first place, he would've enjoyed her being worried about him. "Fine."

"Fine! I'm driving you home."

Jameson would've protested, but when they stood, he wasn't steady on his feet.

*Dammit, if she didn't likely give me a concussion.*

# CHAPTER 8

*Daisy*

Daisy pulled to a stop in front of a florist shop close to Main Street. Jameson had given her directions to his apartment, then promptly closed his eyes and shut her out.

*Does he live here?*

She leaned over the steering wheel to get a better look at the building. It was a two-story brick structure sporting a faux façade embellished with Art Deco elements. On the first-story windows, someone had hand-painted flowers. It was . . . cute. Not what she would've expected out of his apartment. But rentals in the historic part of town were prime real estate. If something came open, you took it, or you'd lose out.

Shrugging, she glanced over at him. "I think we're here."

He opened his eyes and sat up, stifling a groan. "Yeah, thanks."

She quickly unbuckled and scrambled out of the car when he reached for the door. She met him just as he climbed out of her little Honda. "Let me help you."

"I'm fine, Daisy." He ignored her offer of help and headed for an unmarked door to the right of the main storefront. He opened it, and it led up to two apartments on the second floor of the building.

She glared at his back, thinking he was far from 'fine' but restrained herself from commenting as he started up the staircase. She stayed right behind him, ready to offer support should he prove her right and lose his balance.

Though his pace was slow, he didn't stumble, and some of the worry she'd felt started to ease. Jameson's door was on the right at the top of the staircase. She hovered as he dug in his coat pocket for keys. When he'd retrieved them, he swayed slightly.

Before she could move to help him, he slapped a hand against the doorframe for balance. She gritted her teeth and waited. In the quiet of the empty building, his breathing was heavy enough for her to hear, and she knew he was in more pain than he was letting on.

Finally, he pushed off the frame and put the key in the lock. When he entered the apartment, she followed. Despite being a small unit, it had a spacious open-plan living area. The sitting room bled into the kitchen, and all that separated them was a folding table.

He turned around to shut the door and seemed surprised to find her there.

"Don't even think about it. I'm taking a look at your head."

She grabbed his arm and dragged him to the folding table that served as his dining set.

Pulling a chair out, she pushed him into it. "Sit."

When he complied and didn't argue with her, she frowned. His head must truly be hurting him. She flipped on the kitchen lights, and he groaned, shutting his eyes.

After she shed her coat, she started opening drawers, searching for a towel and a first-aid kit. She found a dishcloth and wet it at the sink.

"James, I'm going to clean the wound, okay?"

Opening his eyes, he sighed. "Fine." Propping his arms on the table, he leaned forward to give her better access.

She swallowed a gasp when she got a good look at the injury. Dried blood matted the hair around the cut, staining it a dark rust color. She hoped it looked worse than it was. The blood had dripped down his neck and beneath his jacket, likely wetting the shirt underneath. As gently as she could, she wiped it away with the washcloth.

His hands had clenched into fists by the time she finished.

"Well, it's not as bad as it looked. It's just a scrape, but I already feel a bump forming. Do you have a first-aid kit?" She breathed a sigh of relief that he didn't need stitches.

"In the bathroom. I'll get it." He tried to rise, but she stopped him with a firm push to his shoulders.

"No. Stay put. I'll get it. Where is it?" She didn't want him moving around more than he had to.

"Under the sink." Jameson waved in the direction of the hallway.

Daisy walked down it. There were only two doors, so she had a fifty-fifty chance of picking the right one. She started with the one on the left. *Bingo.*

The bathroom was small but updated. A glass-front shower took up most of the space. There was a small washer/dryer combo right as you walked in. She ignored that, pushing discarded towels aside to open the dark wood vanity.

Apart from a few cleaning supplies, the only thing in there was toilet paper—no first-aid kit. Determined to find it, she started opening drawers. She found acetaminophen and a box of bandages and grabbed them. If he had alcohol, they'd make do.

When she returned to the kitchen, Jameson had laid his head on his arms and appeared to be asleep.

She lightly touched his shoulder. "James, I didn't see a first-aid kit. But I've got band-aids and pain meds."

"Fine." He grumbled without raising his head.

She set the supplies down on the table next to him and went in search of a glass to get him some water. After the third cabinet, she'd found the right one.

"Here, take two of these." Daisy fished out two pills for the headache she knew he had and handed him the glass of water.

"Thanks." He sat up slowly and took the medicine.

Frowning at his wound, she asked, "Would the kit be somewhere else? I'd like to put some alcohol on the cut before I bandage it."

He frowned at her, then waved his hand at the kitchen sink. "Yeah, under the sink."

She opened her mouth to retort that he'd just told her it was under the *bathroom* sink, but then it occurred to her he was confused.

*Oh, shoot! Isn't that a sign of concussion?*

Without saying a word, she walked to the sink and opened the under cabinet. She let out a shaky breath. There was the little red bag.

Carrying it back to the table, she opened it to find alcohol wipes and a better bandage than the ones she'd brought from the bathroom.

"This is going to sting a little." She held her breath as she pressed the alcohol wipe to the cut.

Jameson came alive then. He inhaled sharply. Letting it out, he muttered a string of curses.

She blew on the wound and then placed a bandage over it. "All done, you big baby."

She moved from behind him to find him scowling at her. Not fazed by it, she tugged at the collar of his jacket. "You probably want to take this off and change your shirt. There's blood on it."

He stood and headed for the hallway, presumably to his bedroom.

"Do you need my—"

"No."

He didn't turn around at her question, and Daisy rolled her eyes at his back.

*What a stubborn, macho caveman! If he falls over in there . . .*

She huffed out a breath. Nothing she could do about it.

Remembering her own injury, she propped her foot on the chair Jameson vacated to look at her knee. Her black stockings were in the way if she wanted to clean it out.

Knowing her thigh highs were garbage now anyway, she

hiked up her uniform to pull them down. She had the second one halfway down her thigh when Jameson walked back in.

They both froze, their gazes colliding. A tingling sensation swept up her neck and across her face. She wasn't one to blush, but something in his eyes made her skin heat. There was zero chance she could look away.

His intense stare held her captive as he took one step, then another, to close the distance between them. When his hands covered hers on her thigh, she sucked in a sharp breath.

"Let me help you." His voice was husky, and the sound of it made her knees go weak.

His eyes moved down her leg as they drew the stocking off together. Her skin flushed as he studied her, and she began to feel overly warm. The act had been so simple, yet so erotic. She couldn't speak—afraid to say anything that might make him stop.

Without a word, he began to tend her wound. She barely felt the sting of the alcohol as he wiped it over her knee. Her body trembled, but it had nothing to do with pain. The feel of his hands on her was everything. She wanted more.

When he blew on the scrape, a shiver ran through her, and she couldn't help the moan that escaped.

At the sound, his eyes shot to hers. They were darker and pulsed with need.

She held her breath, hoping, praying that he'd kiss her. When he stood, she lowered her leg and straightened. His gaze held her trapped, and she watched him struggle against the decision.

Impatient with need, she blinked and crushed her lips to his. He groaned and cupped her elbows—to pull her closer or push her away, she wasn't sure. But he did neither as she deepened the kiss.

It wasn't the gentle caress of a first date. It was a hot, wet exploration that spoke of hunger long denied. Their tongues parried and sparred, making her head spin. She grabbed his waist and held on as they sampled the taste of each other.

He moved his hands to her hair and pulled out the ponytail she wore. She felt more than heard his guttural rumble of satisfaction as he captured the loose strands in his fists. Her hands fisted in his shirt, and her head fell back as his mouth moved across her jaw and down her neck. She was breathing heavily, and with each breath, her chest met his. They were fused together, and yet she wanted more.

With trembling hands, she started to lift off Jameson's shirt. His hands remained in her hair as he sucked on her neck, and she couldn't lift it more than halfway.

"Help me, James." Her voice was breathy over her racing heart.

Before she'd realized what was happening, Jameson stopped kissing her and pushed her back to arm's length.

He turned away from her, his chest heaving as much as hers.

*Why did he stop?* Daisy stared, confused, while she waited for him to say something—anything.

She stepped toward him, and he growled, "Don't."

Her eyes widened. The warmth he'd built in her

evaporated as the frost from his tone turned her insides to ice. Hugging her arms across her chest, she blinked against the tears that threatened to fall. She'd been a fool.

Taking a deep breath to calm herself, she spoke. "I think you have a concussion, and I'm not leaving you alone. Unless you've changed your mind about the hospital?"

He finally looked at her. "No."

She nodded matter-of-factly. "That's settled then. Excuse me."

She rushed past him for the bathroom. Closing the door behind her, she leaned against it as a sob escaped. His rejection of her compounded the emotions she'd fought against all day. She'd been harassed, badgered, and teased by almost everyone who'd come into the diner.

But not by Jameson. He'd been her one hope of getting out of this. She should never have let her desire for him complicate the situation.

*Clearly.* Her face twisted on the sour thought. Anger at herself as much as at him flooded her and dried up her tears.

She moved to look at herself in the mirror over the sink. She'd known she wasn't his type. Looking at the mess he'd made of her long, dark hair, she combed her fingers through it. She wasn't blonde or petite, and that's all he'd dated in high school.

She splashed cold water on her face and sighed. At least he wouldn't be able to tell she'd been crying. Her skin was the even bronze color it always was.

After another calming breath, she prepared herself to face him. They'd been friends, so they would stay friends.

She'd make sure he recovered from his head injury, and then he would help her figure out how to prove her innocence.

She could handle that, couldn't she?

# CHAPTER 9

*Jameson*

Jameson stared after Daisy. Damn, he'd screwed up. He grabbed at his hair in frustration and cursed when it made the throbbing in his head worse. How long did it take acetaminophen to kick in anyway? Not that he'd felt the headache a moment ago. No, he'd been much more focused on feeling with a different head.

*Dammit! How could he be so stupid?*

Daisy had disappeared into the bathroom, and he didn't blame her. With what he'd just done, he'd like to get away from himself, too. But he couldn't leave it like that with her.

Shaking his head, Jameson walked to the bathroom door. He raised his hand to knock and heard her sob. The sound tore at his insides.

Great, he was a regular asshole who'd made her cry. He'd seen how worn out she looked from dealing with all the gossip today. Now, he'd gone and made things worse.

Lowering his hand, he decided to give her some space, and then he'd . . . what? Apologize?

*For touching the smooth, satin skin of her thigh? For kissing her like he was a dying man, and she was his last meal? For getting lost in the heady earthiness of her scent? For thinking about hiking those long legs around his waist and taking her hard and fast on his dining table?*

Fuck, he was getting turned on again.

The bathroom door opened, and Daisy paused in the doorway, raising an eyebrow at him.

He cleared his throat. "I was just about to knock. Um—" He searched her face, but she didn't look upset. "I was going to ask, do you want to order a pizza for dinner?"

"Pizza would be great."

"Great." His brows drew together as he stared at her. *Had* she been crying? She certainly seemed fine now.

*Is she mad? No, you know when Daisy's mad at you.* She was . . . calm. Surprisingly, calm. It worried him.

"You should probably let me out of the bathroom so we can order it." She smiled teasingly.

Jameson blinked. "Right. Sorry." He moved aside, and she brushed past him.

"Daisy, wait." He grabbed her arm to stop her, and she stiffened. Loosening his grip, he turned her around so he could see her face. "Look, I'm sorry. I shouldn't have started that."

He thought he saw a flash of anger in her bright blue eyes, but it was gone as quickly as it appeared.

"You know what? Water under the bridge." She shrugged, and he released her arm. "We're friends, right?"

He nodded, but he wasn't so sure of that. He didn't have any friends he wanted to kiss more than he wanted to take his next breath.

"Okay. Then, as my friend, I need you to help me figure out how to get out of this mess, preferably before it goes to trial."

At her mention of his helping her, Jameson flashed back to her plea for help when she'd been trying to take his clothes off. As it had then, it cooled his blood. He was supposed to be helping her prove her innocence, *not* satisfy his own needs. "I can do that."

"Good."

He frowned as she walked away. There was a sinking feeling in his stomach as though he'd missed an opportunity he wouldn't get another chance at.

* * * *

*Daisy*

Later, after they'd gorged themselves on a large pepperoni with extra cheese, Daisy wandered around Jameson's living room. She'd made him recline on the worn-in leather couch with an ice pack on his head when he'd complained the pain meds weren't working.

She took in the boxing bag with a smirk. Once she'd gotten over the tears earlier, she realized she didn't know whether he had a girlfriend. She'd had a moment of panic when she'd thought that had been why he'd pushed her away.

Noticing the bag, she didn't think so. At least, not one

that lived with him.

No, definitely not, judging by the state of the bathroom. Besides, she'd have heard through Dillon if he did. More likely, Jameson was a "love 'em and leave 'em" kind of guy.

*Good.* She nodded absently. Because she wasn't that kind of girl, even if she had been his type.

"Do you want the TV on?" she asked over her shoulder. The monstrous thing hung on the wall across from the couch and had to be 70 inches or more. She had a television, but hers was, what, 46 inches? And that was plenty big enough.

"No. No noise." He closed his eyes and propped his feet up on the scarred coffee table in front of the sofa. She almost felt sorry for him—almost.

Perhaps it was petty, but she was still upset enough that she was glad he had a headache. The man was sorry—*Sorry!*—that they'd kissed. She huffed out a breath and shot a glare in his direction. If she hadn't already cracked his skull, she'd have likely taken a swing at it.

*But he does look kind of miserable lying there.*

With a sigh, Daisy relented; he *had* already helped her with her case. Over dinner, he'd told her about the judge who issued the warrant and his plan to follow up on it.

Grateful that she at least had his professional assistance, she went to sit on the other end of the couch with him. "James, I appreciate you don't want the TV on, but can we talk?" Silence wasn't her forte, and she was starting to go stir-crazy.

He cracked open an eye. "Sure." His answer was hesitant, as though he feared what she might have to say.

She grinned, thankful he'd given in. "How'd you do it? Yesterday, with the arraignment? Blair said that, with it being a Sunday, the DA wouldn't even look at my case until the next morning."

She'd been so relieved at the time that she didn't think to ask, but her curious mind hadn't let her forget. If there were something unanswered, she'd always raise the question.

He gave a slight shrug as the color rose on his cheeks. "I convinced the clerk it couldn't wait."

She studied him carefully. He was looking everywhere but at her until it occurred to her why.

"The clerk was a woman, wasn't she?"

He met her gaze, and his eyes were carefully blank. "So?"

She smirked. His cool demeanor wasn't fooling anyone. "What did you have to promise her to secure my early release?"

"Nothing! Geez, Daisy." His voice turned gruff. "Who do you think I am?"

*That's a good question.*

But it was a question she didn't have the answer to. Her lips pursed at the thought.

"I don't know. I don't really know you anymore, James. And I seem to remember you ran through a string of blondes when you were in high school."

"There wasn't a string," he muttered.

"No?" She goaded. Because she remembered it differently.

"No." He sat up and faced her.

The ice pack lay forgotten on the cushion behind him. Though her fingers itched to pick it up and put it back on his head, she ignored the urge. If he wanted his headache to go away, he'd remember it.

"My turn to ask a question." His eyes were bright, which she took as a good sign. He'd seemed okay during dinner, but that little nugget of worry hadn't left her.

Curious about what he wanted to know, she nodded. "Okay, go ahead."

"What'd you do all those years you were gone?"

She blinked in surprise. "Oh." She hadn't expected him to care about that. "Nothing exciting. I had plans to." She shrugged. "After college, I wanted to travel, but I don't know; something always seemed to come up or made me change direction. I spent the last few years in Chicago as a personal assistant before I moved back. I guess it just took me a while to figure out what I wanted to do."

"Nothing wrong with that." He smiled, and kindness glinted in his eyes. He seemed more relaxed with her now, almost like old times.

"Okay, my turn." She had to know, or it'd drive her crazy. Taking a deep breath, she let it out slowly.

*You can do this, Daisy.*

"Why did you kiss me back?" she asked softly.

He gave a heavy sigh and looked away.

As she waited, a pit formed in her stomach. She might dread the answer, but she needed it all the same.

When his eyes met hers again, the intensity was back. A storm raged in their blue depths. It threatened to wash over her in tumultuous waves like the sea trying to swallow a ship. She held her breath, unable to look away.

"Because I've wanted to since you moved back to town almost two years ago, and I couldn't resist any longer."

Her eyes widened at his admission. *Did he really just say that?*

Her heart pounded against her ribs so hard she worried they might crack. When she found her voice, it came out breathy. "But . . . you've avoided me. Why would you do that if you wanted to kiss me?"

Another long sigh. "Because you're off-limits."

His words were a sucker punch that knocked the wind out of her.

"What? Why?" Confusion grew into a knot in her chest that was slowly squeezing, threatening to cut off her air supply. She rubbed at it, but it didn't soothe the tightening.

His eyes followed the movement. "You're Dillon's sister. How do you think he'd like me kissing you?" His voice was flat in resignation, which only served to set her temper alight.

*Seriously? That's his argument?*

She narrowed her eyes at Jameson. "Why would Dillon care? He doesn't have a say in my relationships."

"It's different for guys. We just . . . can't cross that line." His jaw clenched so hard it could have cracked stone, and he looked away from her.

His view of her as 'off-limits' was utterly juvenile. It was enough to send her over the edge.

"You sound ridiculous! We're not in high school anymore, James." Her voice was sharper than she'd intended, but this whole situation had her agitated and annoyed.

She narrowed her eyes at him and pressed her lips together as she waited for an answer. The rope she'd been teetering on snapped when he continued to ignore her. "Fine! Let's call Dillon right now and ask him."

At that, his eyes flared. "No," he growled at her. "If you get ahold of your brother, that's the last thing we need to tell him. Or have you forgotten that you're facing criminal charges?"

She sucked in a sharp breath and turned away, blinking rapidly against tears that threatened to fall at his harsh reminder. "I'm going to my apartment to pick up a few things. Get some rest if you can. I'll be back to check on you in a little while."

*And make sure you wake up normally, even if you don't deserve it.*

He winced. "Daisy, I—"

"No arguing!" She needed space, not more of his apologies.

Rising, she deliberately didn't look at him as she went to put on her coat and grabbed her purse. She'd done it again, let her feelings for this man supersede everything else. There were more important things than how Jameson felt towards her to worry about, and the clock was ticking. She had three weeks before the preliminary hearing. If there were any hope of getting the charges dropped, they'd have to find a way to prove her innocence before then.

But first, she had to make sure his symptoms didn't worsen. Then, she needed to figure out who put the drugs in her apartment. If the judge was connected, it would mean she was facing a bigger battle than she'd thought. A battle she'd need Jameson's help with.

About to leave, she glanced at him over her shoulder. He'd already shut her out and reclined back on the couch.

The distance he insisted on putting between them was slicing fragments from her heart. She hoped there would be enough left when this was all over.

Impulse had her opening her mouth, not wanting to leave angry. But he'd dismissed her, so she ignored it, turned the lock, and walked out the door.

# CHAPTER 10

*Jameson*

Jameson's eyes flew open as the door closed behind Daisy, and his hands clenched into fists. He glanced at the punching bag, desperate to hit something, but he knew it would only make the pain in his head worse.

Pain that was morphing him into a complete asshole. Twice in the last few hours, that's how many times he'd made her cry.

A fact he could have avoided if he hadn't told her the truth. What had possessed him? Some errant hope that things could be different—that he could have something with Daisy?

He didn't want to hurt her, but if it was the only way to keep her at a distance . . .

When an ache spread through his chest, he rubbed at the space above his heart.

It was the right course of action, then. Wasn't it?

*Or is she right? Am I being stupid, holding onto something that only made sense in high school?*

He and Dillon had been a united front against any losers who'd come sniffing around Daisy and later his own younger siblings. But it's not like they had ever officially said they wouldn't date each other's sisters. It was just understood—it went without saying.

He gave a sharp nod and winced when it sent a shockwave of pain radiating from the base of his skull. Clenching his eyes shut against the assault, he cursed. He needed another acetaminophen.

When the wave reduced from stabbing to stinging, he opened his eyes, glancing toward the folding table in his kitchen. He could see the tiny medication bottle sitting there—his salvation.

Debating whether it was worth it to risk the pain of moving for the relief of the medicine, Jameson wished he hadn't sent Daisy away.

Because he had. It was *his* fault she'd left and wasn't here to help him.

Grimacing, he sat up slowly, careful not to jar his head. When the movement didn't cause any new agony, he exhaled in relief.

He could do this. Gathering confidence, he stood. But that was as far as he got. The world tilted, and he fell back on the couch with a growl.

*Great. Just fucking great.*

He broke out in a sweat, suffering through a new wave of pain at the impact. Closing his eyes, he resigned himself to the fact he wasn't going anywhere until she returned.

*If* she returned.

He wouldn't blame her for leaving him to manage it alone, not after how he'd treated her.

He wished things were different—that he could go back to that moment when she'd been ready to strip his clothes off. He'd help her, then return the favor. They could be in his bed right now with her lying in his arms.

*Not helpful.* He berated himself.

Besides, no matter how much he wanted that, it would never happen. She was still his best friend's sister, and he wouldn't risk losing the only family he had left in this town. Because that's what Dillon was—his brother. Even if they didn't share blood.

*Blood.* His stomach churned with a memory.

He hadn't told Daisy about the phone call he'd received when he was at the diner. There was no reason to burden her with it when he had more questions than answers. And despite what he might feel in his gut, he had no proof it was related to her case. So, he'd sit on it . . . for now, at least until he could get in touch with Dillon.

Out of habit, he reached for the phone he kept in his pants pocket. Finding it empty, he cursed.

Thankfully, the one Daisy destroyed when she'd sent them both flying into the pavement had been his work-issued phone. His personal cell was out of reach in his bedroom. He debated trying to stand again but decided against it.

Closing his eyes, he resolved to get a new phone from the station tomorrow. Then, he'd start following up on what little leads he had.

Going over what information he'd gathered about

Daisy's case and his plan to visit the judge in the morning, Jameson drifted off to sleep.

* * * *

*Daisy*

Daisy pulled up in front of the florist shop and blew out a noisy breath. She'd only been gone an hour, and it hadn't been long enough. Her stomach jumped with nerves at the thought of seeing Jameson again. She'd been tempted to leave him alone for the rest of the night because, obviously, that was what he wanted.

Her dark blue eyes went hard as she glared at his building. If he weren't injured, she would've—gladly.

He'd hurt her, and for what? Some silly, misconceived notion about betraying a bond with her brother?

Her body flushed with the heat of her anger as she thought about it, and her nails bit into her palms.

*Such a stupid reason!*

She slammed her way out of the car with her outrage on a simmer. The sound echoed in the quiet of the evening and had her scanning the street.

Despite the late hour, it was lit well enough by overhead lamps that she could see all the way to the corner. A shiver ran up her neck as she scanned the historic buildings, but she wasn't cold. She'd changed out of her diner uniform into the more sensible outfit of jeans and a sweater.

Frowning at the sensation of being watched, Daisy glanced around, but no one was there. The street was empty of people, and the few cars she noted were dark—no lights or exhaust. The air was cool enough that the fumes would've been visible had one been running.

*Odd.* Shaking it off, she entered the building and started up the stairs to the second-floor apartments.

She stopped in front of Jameson's door and groaned quietly in frustration. In her haste to leave, she'd forgotten to ask him for a key. He'd told her his landlady lived next door, but she would only use her as a last resort.

Raising her hand, Daisy knocked quietly on his door, hoping she wouldn't disturb the woman.

When he didn't answer, she tried again, her knock a little louder. "James, it's me. Open up," she whisper-yelled and felt ridiculous.

She counted to five, but there was still no answer. Losing her temper, Daisy pounded on the door, flinching at how loud it was. "James, open the door!"

She tensed, expecting the landlady to come out shrieking at her, but nothing happened.

No landlady and no Jameson.

Her brow wrinkled as she stared at the door. Was he deliberately not answering? Had he fallen asleep?

*What if he couldn't wake up?*

Her throat constricted. He was concussed. She shouldn't have left him.

Her breathing started to accelerate, but she shook her head, refusing to panic. There had to be a spare key somewhere. He didn't have a doormat to hide it under, but what about . . .

Daisy reached for the top of the doorframe.

*Darnit!* She wasn't quite tall enough.

Standing on her tiptoes, she tried again. She stretched, and her fingers could just fold over the ledge. Grunting with the effort, she ran her hand along the top of the door. At the touch of something small and cold, she let out a sigh of relief.

But she still needed to get the key. She pushed with her fingertips until she had it tipped off the ledge, then she caught it as it fell and grinned triumphantly.

Daisy's grin disappeared when she opened the door. The light was still on in the kitchen, and it shone over Jameson, who was on the couch where she'd left him.

She rushed to his side as all manner of terrible things ran through her mind.

*Is he alive?*

*Is he still breathing?*

*Please be breathing!*

"James!" She crouched beside him on the couch and laid her head on his chest. He had a heartbeat.

*Thank goodness!*

Her muscles went weak, and she slumped beside him. That had scared her more than she was willing to admit. Taking a calming breath, she sat up and looked at him.

He was relaxed in sleep, and with his hair falling into his face, his features were softer. She smiled and swept the curls off his forehead. The soft strands felt like velvet in her hand.

She traced the outline of his jaw and admired the tiny cleft in his chin. His lips were so close. She had the sudden urge to kiss them. As if Jameson were some fairytale prince, she'd wake him with true love's kiss.

Daisy blinked. *True love?* Was she in love with him?

That was silly; she didn't even know him anymore. More likely, she was obsessed with her crush on him as a girl. And that was so not important at the moment. She rolled her eyes at herself.

Determined to stop mooning over the man, she felt the back of his head. The swelling was worse. She frowned as she spotted the ice pack on the other end of the couch.

*He should've kept it iced!*

Tempted to shake him awake, she stopped herself. That would likely make his symptoms worse.

Trying another tactic, she bent down and spoke directly in his ear. "James, you stubborn mule. If you don't wake up, I'm going to throw water in your face."

The idea had occurred to her, but she hoped she wouldn't have to resort to it. She sat back, but he remained sound asleep.

*Okayyy, let's try this. It shouldn't bother his head.*

She tapped repeatedly on his chest. "Come on, James. I need you to wake up!"

When he still didn't stir, she glanced at his mouth again. Would it work? She leaned in.

Her lips hovering above his, she spoke, "James, if you don't wake up right now, I'm going to kiss you."

His breaths washed over her in an even rhythm; he stayed asleep.

She hesitated. Was she actually going to do this? It seemed unfair somehow when she knew he didn't want her to kiss him.

But did it matter if she was trying to ensure he was

okay? Did that give her the right?

She grimaced. *No. It didn't.*

It was going to be water then. She was about to pull back when she felt his hand in her hair. Her eyes shot to his, but they were closed.

"James," she whispered, unsure what was happening.

His lips curled in a soft smile as he ran his fingers through her hair. "Daisy."

She froze when his arms came around her and squeezed. "Yes. I'm here. I need you to wake up," she said, her words muffled by his chest.

"I'm awake," he protested, though sleep colored his voice.

Her breath caught at the sexy sound. She was in his arms again, and the feeling was torture as much as it was ecstasy, knowing he wasn't fully aware of what he was doing.

She inhaled deeply, savoring his woodsy scent—the masculine, oaky smell that would forever remind her of him. She'd at least have that if he weren't willing to give her anything else.

With a small shake of her head, she demanded, "All the way up."

"No, let's stay in bed." His sleepy request had warmth pooling in her belly, and nerve endings that had already started stirring tingled in anticipation.

She gulped against the sensation. She'd like to be in whatever dream he was having, but this was not helping her focus on the task at hand. The only other thing she could think of was to—

"Ow!" His body jerked at her pinch, and he came fully awake. "Daisy?" he asked as his eyes slowly focused on her.

She sighed in relief—or disappointment; she wasn't sure. As much as she wanted to make sure he could wake up without issue, she wouldn't have minded a few more minutes of sleepy Jameson.

"I'd say good morning, but it's probably closer to ten. You were only out an hour. How's your head?"

"My head?" He moved to sit up and winced. "Right, my head. It's throbbing."

"Stay put." She grabbed the ice pack off the couch. "I'll get you another one of these and more meds."

When she returned from the kitchen, he hunched over with his head resting in his hands. Her heart gave a little pang at seeing him like that. "Is it still that bad?"

He looked up at her. The pain was there in the tightness of his eyes, but there was something else, regret, maybe? He blinked, and it was gone.

Clearing his throat, he answered, "I think the medicine wore off."

"Here, this will help." She handed him more acetaminophen and a glass of water.

He downed the pills, and she wondered how to broach the sleeping situation. As far as she could tell, this was a one-bedroom apartment. While she usually wouldn't mind sleeping on the couch, Jameson's worn-out leather one didn't look comfortable. Plus, she would have to wake him up every few hours.

It would make more sense if they slept together. But she wasn't sure how to convince him of that.

Her eyes looked far away as she thought about it, and he noticed. "What is it?"

"Hmm," she focused on him. He'd set the glass aside and was staring at her. "Oh, um, here's your ice pack."

She shoved it at him, and he took it with a raised eyebrow. "Thanks."

"We should probably get some sleep." She tried a bland smile to mask the butterflies in her stomach.

"You can take the bed. I'll sleep out here," he offered like she'd known he would.

She tried to keep her voice even when she told him, "I don't think that's a good idea."

He opened his mouth to protest, but she raised a hand and cut him off. "Hear me out. You're already uncomfortable because of the pain. You need to sleep where you'll get the most rest."

He cocked his head at her in disbelief. "You want to sleep on the couch?"

She propped her hands on her hips. "No, of course not. We'll sleep together. In your bed." With the challenge issued, she waited, ready for his rebuttal.

When he spoke, she blinked in surprise. "Fine."

*Excuse me?* He agreed with her. Daisy squinted at him, sure she'd misheard. "Fine?"

"I'm tired. I'd much rather sleep in my own bed when my head feels like someone's going at it with a jackhammer. Trust me. I don't have the energy to argue with you." He moved to stand up, and she was there to help him.

"Are you still getting dizzy?" She placed his arm over her

shoulders for balance.

He didn't answer immediately but stood, feet planted to steady himself. "No, just the headache now."

"Well, that's good, at least." A slow smile lit her face. "Let's get you to bed, big guy."

He grunted but didn't pull away from her support as she helped him down the hall to his bedroom.

She flipped the light switch, and he groaned when the overhead lamp turned on.

"Sorry, that is pretty bright. Just keep your eyes closed."

The bedroom wasn't huge, but the lack of furniture made it feel more spacious than it was. A low bed took up most of the area. Next to it was a nightstand with a bedside lamp. That was it as far as furnishings went.

"You're a real minimalist, aren't you," she mumbled.

After helping him onto the bed, she turned on the bedside lamp, letting its soft glow light the room. Then, she flipped off the overhead switch.

Staring down at him, she chewed her lip. "Can you get undressed, or do you nee—"

"I've got it, Daisy," he barked at her.

"Of course you do," she muttered. More loudly, she announced, "I'll give you a few minutes," and stepped out, closing the bedroom door behind her.

She changed into the pajamas she'd brought, a pair of soft terry shorts, and a well-worn t-shirt from her college days, then got ready for bed. Knowing he'd likely need more of it, she poured two glasses of water and grabbed the bottle of acetaminophen off the kitchen table.

When she'd returned to the bedroom door, there was no way she could open it, juggling water glasses and a bottle of pills. "James, I'm sorry, but can you open the door? My hands are full."

Thankfully, this time, he hadn't fallen asleep. He opened the door, and a wave of desire washed over her.

She stared, lost in admiring his bare torso. There was a defined line where his shoulders met his chest. She'd never met another man with shoulders as broad as Jameson. They'd been impressive under clothes, but uncovered, they were glorious. She licked her lips and thought about sinking her teeth into the ridge of muscles that topped them.

*What would he taste like?*

"I can take that." He reached his hand towards her, and she finally tore her gaze from his chest to meet his eyes.

*Take what?*

His hand closed around one of the glasses she clutched, and she swallowed.

*Right. Take the glass.*

He turned away from her, and she followed him into the room, trying and failing not to stare at his back. It was as enticing as the front. There was another defined line. This one ran down the middle, showing off the muscles that flanked it on either side.

How did a body have that many ridges and planes? She could spend all day and not explore them all. Her fingertips tingled with the need to trace them.

He set the glass on the nightstand and turned off the lamp.

With the room plunged into darkness, she regathered her wits. It was pitch-black without the light, so she had to feel her way to the nightstand by shuffling her feet. She heard the bed shift as he climbed into it.

Once she'd set her glass of water and the medicine down, she reached out a hand, feeling for the bed. She gasped when she connected with Jameson's chest.

"What are you doing?" His voice didn't sound angry, just weary.

"Sorry! It's so dark. I'm trying not to stub a toe."

"Here." He grabbed the hand she hadn't removed from his chest and pulled her down onto the bed.

She sucked in a sharp breath when she found herself splayed on top of him. Everywhere her skin met his, she felt a spark.

Before she had more than a second to enjoy it, he grunted and rolled her off. "Goodnight, Daisy."

Her breathing was a little unsteady, and her voice came out breathier than she would've liked. "Goodnight, James."

Every nerve ending in her body had woken up. She closed her eyes, and the sight of him in nothing but gym shorts appeared behind her eyelids.

Muscles. He was all muscles: his shoulders, his arms, his abs, his legs. The man's body was flawless.

*How on earth am I supposed to get any sleep lying next to that?*

# CHAPTER 11

*Jameson*

Jameson awoke at the beeping of his alarm. On autopilot, he reached out to tap the snooze button. Slowly, his brain registered his surroundings. There was a warm weight on his chest, and he reached for it, confused when his hand met something soft and silky. Opening his eyes to a slit, he blinked against the early morning light streaming in through the cracks in the blinds. Then, he lifted his head slightly and spotted Daisy, fast asleep and curled into his side. Her head lay on his chest, and her hair splayed over his arm.

*Am I still dreaming?*

When the events of yesterday came back to him, he stiffened.

*Real. This is real.*

Daisy was in his bed.

He could smell her. The same musky scent that drove him crazy yesterday. It was both sweet and spicy and made him want to taste her again. He felt her breasts pressed against his side through the thin t-shirt she wore.

Stifling a groan, he recalled the tiny shorts she'd put on. They did nothing to hide the smooth length of her legs— legs he wanted her to wrap around him.

*Fuck!*

This was bending the rules, if not breaking them. He had to get away from her.

Careful not to wake her, he slowly edged out from under her. She made a small sound of disapproval when his chest was no longer supporting her, but she resettled and stayed asleep.

Glancing down at her, he noticed the faint circles under her eyes. She had to be tired. Three? Four times? He'd lost track, but she'd done as she'd said she would and woken him up every couple of hours.

He appreciated her concern but didn't think it had been necessary. They'd both be struggling today with the lack of decent rest.

After a lingering look, he shook himself. *Not yours.*

Backing away, he tried to tread softly as he gathered clothes from the closet, wanting to let her sleep while she could.

He showered, dressed, and made coffee in record time. The knowledge of Daisy and her tiny shorts asleep in his bed was more than he could handle right now. He was hoping to get out of the apartment before she woke up.

He'd scrawled a note on a paper napkin, letting her know he was off to work. Then he'd downed a cup of coffee and more pain meds. The ice or time had done the job on the swelling, but he still felt stiff from the injury.

He panicked when he was ready to leave, remembering his car was still at the diner. Changing tactics, he called the station for a pickup.

Figuring he'd wait downstairs, he placed his mug in the sink and shrugged on his jacket.

He was halfway to the door when he heard footsteps behind him. *Dammit.*

Dread and anticipation warred within him at the thought of turning around and seeing her in those shorts.

"Well, at least you seem to be recovered from your injury." Her voice was thick with sleep, but when he turned around, her crossed arms and narrowed eyes told him she wasn't too sleepy to be upset with him.

"Good morning."

He struggled to keep his eyes trained on her face as she walked toward him. When she stopped only a foot away, he gulped.

Her scent wafted over him, and with her hair all mussed from sleep, he was having trouble forming coherent sentences. "Sleep. I was trying to let you sleep."

"You probably should've turned the alarm off then."

Her smile was hard, and her hands had moved to her hips. The stance stretched the thin t-shirt across her chest, and it took every ounce of strength he had not to stare at her breasts.

*Fuck!* He'd forgotten he'd only hit the snooze button. "Sorry about that."

"Off to work so early?" Even though her voice was pleasant, her eyes flashed their irritation at him.

"Yeah, there's a, ah"—she shifted, and his gaze fell to her unhindered breasts—"car. They're picking me up."

"And you were just going to what? Leave me here without a word?" she challenged.

*Get it together, asshole.*

He swallowed and brought his gaze back to her face. "No. I left you a note."

"A note." The way she said it made it sound like the worst thing he could've done.

"Yeah. Look, Daisy. I . . ." The power call of a police siren caused him to pause. "That's the car. I have to go. You can stay as long as you'd like."

He backed away from her slowly, bracing for an argument. "We'll talk when I'm done with work."

She opened her mouth to say something but closed it with a frown.

He took one last look at her—the sexy hair, the shapely breasts beneath the thin t-shirt, the long, bare legs—and committed it to memory. "See you later, Daisy."

He'd turned away and had his hand on the doorknob when she said, "Goodbye, James."

He hesitated.

The fight had gone out of her tone, and those two little words sounded almost too final. The siren sounded again, and he shook it off. If he was going to help her, he had to leave his apartment. Opening the door, he left her behind.

* * * *

*Daisy*

Daisy stared after Jameson. He was going to leave, just like that? She felt . . . what? What did she feel? Confused? Hurt?

*Empty.*

The hollow in her stomach told her she was empty. She couldn't believe he had planned to leave without saying anything.

*I mean, come on, I didn't have to take care of him, but I did.*

And he didn't even acknowledge it. He thought he could just sneak out of there—no word of thanks—*nothing.*

He could worry about her brother getting mad that they'd kissed but not think Dillon wouldn't tear into him after how he'd just treated her? It made no sense.

*Men, ugh!*

Seething, she stormed into the kitchen in search of coffee. Spotting the note he'd left her, she picked it up.

"Gone to work. Will call later."

*The nerve!* As if she was some hussy he'd spent the night with.

Well, no, sir, he was not getting away with that! She deserved more than two measly sentences. A lot more.

Daisy poured herself a cup of coffee. After she took the first steaming sip, her anger subsided. She was acting as if he'd wronged her. They were just friends; she hardly had the right to act like the jilted girlfriend. She had no claim on him; he could come and go as he pleased.

Frowning over that, she rubbed at the twinge in her chest. She wanted to put a claim on him. Not dating her because of her brother was silly.

*Off-limits.* Daisy rolled her eyes at the word.

She needed to convince Jameson that she was totally *within* limits, but she wasn't sure how. Mulling it over, she took her coffee with her to the bathroom.

After she'd showered and dressed, her head had cleared enough that she knew she needed to talk to Blair and get in touch with her brother, but not about Jameson. No, she was focusing on what was really important—her case.

She did another sweep of the room to ensure she had everything. Packed and ready to go, she stepped out the door at the same time as Jameson's neighbor.

When she turned, she was surprised to find a glamorous blonde woman staring up at her. "Oh!"

*Is this the landlady? Not what I was expecting . . .*

The woman looked about forty and was well-dressed in wedge boots, corduroy pants, and a sleek black cardigan. Daisy's own worn-in jeans and oversized sweater felt frumpy in comparison.

When the woman didn't speak, she offered her hand. "Hi. I'm Daisy."

The landlady glanced at the hand but didn't accept it. "Shelly." Her brown eyes narrowed. "So, you know Jameson?"

Daisy searched the woman's face. Was Shelly worried she had broken in or something? "Yes, we're friends."

"Friends." Her lips pressed together in a thin line.

"Yes, friends." She stared at Shelly, confused by the third-degree she was getting. "I'm sorry, is there a problem?"

Shelly smiled, but it was fake. "No, of course not. Well,

I've got to get to work. I run the flower shop downstairs."

"Okay, nice to meet you." Daisy gave a small wave and waited for the woman to disappear down the stairs.

That was strange. She'd acted . . . *jealous*. Like she'd been upset because a woman was coming out of Jameson's apartment.

*Ewww. James, tell me you didn't sleep with your landlady.*

Daisy rolled her eyes and huffed out a breath. She was going to ask him about that.

* * * *

*Unknown*

The blond's light blue eyes iced over as his man reported the woman had spent the night with the cop. He'd made sure to keep tabs on her, but knowing she was staying with the arresting officer was disconcerting. Plans might have to change if she'd gone to him for help.

When the light caught it, the ring on the blonde man's right hand flashed as he drummed manicured fingers against the expensive leather of his desk chair. Meanwhile, his man droned on.

There were other ways to get what he wanted, he supposed. This new development might not even be a hiccup. Perhaps it even gave him something he could use *against* the woman.

He was a businessman. A calculated one, which meant he always had a backup plan. Usually, more than one.

A sharp grin made his shiny veneers flash, and he

disconnected the call without a word.

The woman was up on criminal charges. Consorting with her arresting officer carried all kinds of implications they could raise in court.

Perhaps the cop had tampered with evidence for her. Or had he been part of her drug scheme all along, helping her to avoid detection?

All he had to do was plant the seed of doubt and watch it grow.

*Yes, this situation can be turned to my advantage, and I know just how to do it.*

# CHAPTER 12

*Jameson*

Jameson pulled into the parking lot of the Dale County courthouse and cursed. It was nearly full. He'd known the place would be busy on a Tuesday. Still, he'd hoped coming by at lunchtime would allow him to wrangle a few minutes with Judge Emerson, who'd issued the search warrant against Daisy.

He'd spent most of the morning studying Emerson, looking for a connection to anything that might explain the judge's involvement in her case. So far, he'd come up empty.

But sometimes, you had to shake things up before the pieces fell into place. And right now, he had a lot of pieces he wasn't sure even fit together.

He pulled into a park and frowned. Puzzles were his thing, but this one had him chasing his tail in multiple directions.

The narcotics unit at the county level was looking into

following the drugs. They'd dusted for fingerprints and come up empty. A fact that frustrated him but gave strength to his conviction that Daisy had been framed. If she'd put the drugs in her apartment, surely her prints would have been on them.

Not that he'd thought she had, but any piece of evidence that worked in their favor was necessary to point out. While narcotics focused on tracing the packaging, he'd reached out to his contact in Chicago to try and track down Daisy's ex.

Jameson needed to know where the man was and whether he was involved. They'd had no luck at Derrick's apartment, but the search was ongoing, especially after the blood they'd found yesterday.

With those pieces of the puzzle on hold, he would focus on whatever information he could get from the judge.

He climbed out of the police cruiser and grumbled as the bright light of the midday sun caused him to squint. The motion had pain shooting through his head.

He'd been popping acetaminophen like candy against a lingering headache from yesterday's funfest, and he'd forgotten his sunglasses in his rush to get out of the apartment this morning.

He shielded his eyes with a hand. At least the rays made the temperature bearable. Not that he minded much. He'd always preferred the winter's cold to summer's heat, and it was a balmy twenty degrees Fahrenheit with not a cloud in the sky.

Hustling past the crowd of people leaving for lunch, he climbed the steps to the courthouse and had a flash of leading Daisy up those same steps.

Had it only been two days ago that he'd been here with her?

It felt like so much had happened since then. And yet, so much less had happened than he'd like.

*No one to blame but yourself there, James.*

She'd been pissed at him this morning. That much was clear, but he hadn't been trying to hurt her. Leaving like that had been purely for self-preservation. Still, he hadn't even thanked her for helping him.

He'd have to make up for that somehow. If he could. He seemed to be stuck with the adage "damned if you do and damned if you don't." There was no win-win here.

The only way to survive the next few weeks was to keep her at arm's length. He'd help her find whoever was framing her, but there would be no touching allowed. And absolutely no sleeping together, even if it didn't involve any sex. His willpower was strong, but it could only hold so long. Especially against those tiny shorts.

Someone cleared their throat behind him; he'd paused in the middle of the walkway. "Sorry."

Shaking himself out of the memory, Jameson climbed the wide marble stairs to the second-floor offices. When he found Judge Emerson's door, he didn't knock. Opening it without waiting for an invitation, he stepped inside.

*Nice digs.*

He'd entered a spacious outer office decorated in deep burgundy wallpaper with dark wood wainscotting. A plush leather couch lined one wall, and a mahogany desk with a startled clerk took up the other.

The young clerk blinked at him from behind horn-rimmed glasses. "Can I help you?"

He glanced at the young man and then at the door directly across from him. That had to be the judge's office.

"I have business with Judge Emerson."

"Do you have an appointment?" The clerk turned to his computer screen.

When he started clicking around with the mouse, Jameson cleared his throat. "Is the judge in?" He didn't want the man searching for a meeting that didn't exist.

"Yes, but he's—"

That was all the confirmation Jameson needed. He strode to the connecting door.

"Sir! Sir! You can't—" The young clerk's voice rose in volume when he realized what he intended.

Pushing the judge's door open, he entered with the clerk on his heels. The judge's chambers were similarly decorated to the anteroom, but it was twice the size with a large window that added natural light.

It streamed in behind the judge, who stood from his seat at a sleek mahogany desk with Jameson's abrupt entry. The judge was probably in his fifties and balding. Another man, a blond, sat across from him, but he didn't turn around.

"Jenkins, what is the meaning of this?" Judge Emerson snapped at his clerk though he stared at Jameson.

"I'm sorry, sir! He just charged in. I tried—"

"That's enough." The judge cut the poor man off. "Who are you?" His dark eyes narrowed at Jameson.

Taking two steps into the room, he paused when the

judge held up a hand. "That's far enough until you explain yourself."

Jameson smiled. He'd try the friendly approach, though alarms were going off in his gut. There was something about the blonde man that had his skin prickling.

"Apologies, Judge Emerson." He pulled out his badge and held it up. "I'm Sergeant Jameson with the Rolling Brook Police." Was it his imagination, or did the judge pale at that? "I was hoping to talk to you in relation to a case I'm working on."

The judge frowned. "Sergeant, if this is about a warrant, there's a proper procedure. You can't just barge in here—"

"Sir," Jameson stopped him. "With all due respect, I'm not asking you to write me a warrant. But I want to talk to you about the one you issued against Daisy Redland."

Yep, the man's skin turned sallow at that. His eyes darted to the blonde man, who stiffened in his seat.

"Look, Sergeant, whatever questions you have, you're barking up the wrong tree." He made a show of reaching for the coat hanging on a rack in the corner behind his desk. "We have a lunch meeting to get to. If you'll excuse us?" The judge shrugged on his coat, and the blond stood.

When he turned around, Jameson's teeth clenched. In two quick strides, he'd cornered the man against the judge's desk. "Chase Sinclair."

"I'm sorry, Sergeant, was it? I don't think I've had the pleasure." His oily voice slithered over Jameson as he extended a hand.

Jameson didn't even look at it. "I thought you were rotting in a jail cell," he growled.

Sinclair had been sentenced on conspiracy charges after he'd provided information to Blair's kidnappers last year. Jameson was out of town and missed the whole ordeal, but Dillon had filled him in.

It still rubbed him the wrong way that he hadn't been there when his friend needed him. So, yeah, he had some unresolved anger, but he'd gladly take it out on this son-of-a-bitch.

"Thankfully, no. That was all a misunderstanding, I'm afraid."

Jameson's jaw set, and he grabbed Sinclair by the lapels. "Well, understand this. You will be if I find out you had anything to do with Daisy Redland's case."

"Stand down, Sergeant, or I'm calling security," Judge Emerson demanded.

"That's all right, Niles," Sinclair spoke to the judge, but he grinned at Jameson.

It was all he could do not to punch the fucker in his smug face.

Sinclair lowered his voice and stared pointedly at Jameson's hands on his jacket. "The Sergeant knows what constitutes assault, though I'd say you're toeing the line here. I may have to complain to your superiors."

On a sigh of disgust, he released the slimy snake. He had no doubts Sinclair was dirty. The kind of dirty that got white-washed with money so frequently it was hard to find the stains.

If Sinclair and Judge Emerson were on a first-name basis, then his instincts about the judge were right. There was no way he didn't have something to do with Daisy's arrest.

"Well, I'd say it was nice meeting you, but . . ." Sinclair trailed off with a chuckle, and Jameson's face flushed in anger.

His hands clenched into fists, and he again contemplated punching the man. Just one quick jab, and he'd break the fucker's nose. It might be worth it. Except, he'd have a hard time helping Daisy if he got suspended.

*Dammit.*

Taking a calming breath, he ignored Sinclair and turned to leave. He frowned at the two security guards flanking the judge's door. He'd been so focused on the blond that he hadn't noticed the clerk leave and return with them, but it didn't matter. He'd gotten all he would here.

As a parting shot, he zeroed in on the judge. "Judge Emerson, I'd be careful of the company you keep. I'd hate to be revisiting you after a complaint of judicial misconduct."

The judge sputtered at that, but he didn't need a response. Nodding to the two guards, he let them lead him out of the building.

* * * *

## Daisy

Coming back to Rolling Brook was supposed to be a fresh start, but it felt like someone wanted to bury her under it. She'd had a plan. To work for a year or two to save money while she completed her MBA. Then, when she got her degree, she'd have a nice nest egg to put towards a down payment on her own business. But now, that plan was flickering in the wind against a chilling new reality—one where she faced years in prison.

Daisy sighed and clutched her cup of coffee as she stared out her tiny kitchen window. She'd spent half the day trying to get ahold of Dillon and the other half discussing case strategy with Blair. It had made her head hurt, and she was tired enough that the caffeine wasn't making a difference. If she hadn't been waiting on Jameson to catch her up on whatever he'd found out today, she'd have already crashed. As it was, a nap on the couch was sounding more and more appealing.

She hoped he had some good news for her because she didn't think she could take any more bad. At least not without some sleep. Yawning, she nearly fell over. She blinked bleary eyes and glanced at the microwave clock—5:30 p.m. Jameson should be done with work by now.

If he didn't call her soon, she was calling him. He wasn't allowed to ignore her. She'd make sure of it.

She'd told Blair about the kiss and Jameson's silly notion of her as "off-limits."

Daisy's face twisted every time she thought of the word. Being a sensible woman, her sister-in-law had agreed with her. Jameson was holding onto something that would only leave both of them frustrated and alone. She and Blair had even chuckled over the folly of men and their caveman sensibilities.

Then they'd debated a different strategy, but as far as Daisy could tell, she had two options. One—seduce Jameson to the point he's willing to forget she's Dillon's sister. Or two—talk to Dillon and convince him to tell Jameson he's not opposed to them having a relationship. Since she couldn't get in touch with Dillon, she was going with option number one. Well, when she didn't feel like death warmed over.

Daisy bobbled her mug and almost spilled the remnants on herself when she heard a knock at her door. Shaking her head at how distracted she was, she placed her cup on the counter and went to answer it.

When she reached the door, she hesitated. Her current situation had made her wary, and she wasn't expecting anyone. Jameson said he'd call, hadn't he? Would he just show up?

"Daisy, it's me. I know you're home." The sound of his voice had her tense muscles relaxing.

With a smile, she opened the door for him.

# CHAPTER 13

*Jameson*

"Hi." Daisy looked as tired as Jameson felt despite the smile she greeted him with. The shadows had lengthened under her eyes, and her usually warm complexion looked wan.

Even so, he couldn't help but smile at the sight of her. "Hi. Can I come in?"

She stepped back, opening the door wide. "Can I get you anything?" she asked after he'd stepped inside.

"No. I'm good."

He headed for the sofa but then thought better of it. He needed to maintain space, and the couch was just too cozy. They could sit at her kitchen table while he told her what he'd found out today.

He took a seat and gestured for her to do the same.

After she sat, she started fiddling with the end of her ponytail. "You've got news?" Her voice was tight, and when he didn't answer right away, she started biting the inside of her lip.

The nervous gesture drew his eye to her sultry mouth—dark and lush like a ripe plum. His thoughts shifted to what it would feel like to kiss her again, to soothe that spot with his tongue.

"James?" Her voice broke into his fantasy.

He blinked and cursed himself as his face started to heat.

Bringing his eyes back to hers, he explained, "Yeah. Some."

He took a deep breath and launched into what happened when he'd visited Judge Emerson.

When he got to the part about Chase Sinclair, Daisy gasped. "We have to tell Jake and Blair!"

"We will. The guy is bad news, Daisy. I don't have proof he's involved in your situation, but my gut tells me he is." His teeth clenched at the thought, and he wished he'd been able to punch the bastard.

At his words, she deflated. "That's the problem. We need proof and soon, *before* time runs out."

He covered the hand she'd rested on the table with one of his own and tried not to focus on how soft and smooth it felt. "We'll find it, Daisy. I promise."

She smiled softly and turned her hand over to clasp his. He stared down at their intertwined fingers and acknowledged he was breaking his own rule by touching her, but he didn't have the heart to pull his hand away. Not when it was clear she needed the comfort.

"There's something else." He felt her tense, so he hurried on, "Narcotics traced the drugs found in your apartment back to a supplier in Chicago. They wanted to question you about it, but I told them I would handle it."

When he'd received the call from the narcotics unit at the county, he'd had to fight hard to get them to agree to let him take the lead. He'd leveraged his relationship with Daisy's brother to convince them she'd be more likely to spill to someone she knew. Thankfully, he'd worn them down. They would've gone over his head to the captain if he hadn't, and she would've been in for another trip to the station.

She blew out a breath, and her eyes searched his. "Okayyy," she drew the word out as she released his hand. Crossing her arms over her chest, she said, "Question me then."

He cleared his throat and moved his hands to his lap. *No more touching.* "Does the name 'The Rook' ring any bells?"

He doubted she ran in the same circles as the Chicago underground, but maybe she'd heard it before. The supplier's code name was well-known, but not his true identity. Chicago police and the DEA had been trying to catch him for years.

"What? Like in chess?" A frown line appeared between her eyes, and his fingers twitched with the urge to smooth it away.

"Yeah. It's the supplier's nickname. I'm guessing you've never heard of it, then?"

She shook her head.

"Okay, well. Either he's framing you or is helping someone else do it. The question I don't have an answer to is why." But he was determined to find out.

She sagged back into her chair. "Yeah, me either."

Not done with the questions, Jameson tried to ignore how tired she looked. "Do you have any enemies you know of?"

"No." She laughed at the idea. "Why would anyone view me as an enemy?"

He didn't find it funny. "You never know . . . maybe there's a jilted lover? A jealous friend? Someone who thinks you wronged them somehow?"

She had smirked and was shaking her head at the notion when she abruptly stopped. Frowning now, she said, "Oh, well, maybe Amber."

"The server at Shug's?" He didn't know much about the woman but would look into it if Daisy thought she might be an issue.

She cringed. "Yes. I snapped at her on Monday."

That surprised him. "Really? What did she do?"

Daisy had a temper. He knew from firsthand experience, but for her to lose her cool with someone at work seemed out of character. The times she'd snapped at him were usually well-warranted. Like when he and Dillon had kicked the shit out of her boyfriend for telling everyone in the locker room, he'd taken her to third base.

She looked away from his gaze and started fiddling with the tip of her ponytail again. "She was being unprofessional, that's all."

There was more to it than that, but he'd let it slide for now. Amber didn't strike him as the kind of person with connections to drug traffickers in Chicago, and if Daisy had only recently snubbed her, it didn't fit that the woman had planned to frame her before that.

"Well, if you think of anyone else, let me know."

He should get going, but he wanted to spend more time with her. He told himself to stand up—to leave, but his body didn't respond.

What if they got dinner—as friends—and talked about the case?

"I will." She looked at him, and he was struck by how worn out she was.

No, she could use a break from the case. They could talk about . . . whatever friends talked about. He wanted them to get to know each other again as adults—adults who were friends.

*Yeah, try saying 'friends' a few more times, jackass. You're not convincing anyone.*

"So, what do we do next?" Her question broke him out of his thoughts.

"I've got to talk to Chicago. See if they can help us with 'The Rook'." *And with Derrick.*

With the drugs leading back to the city, Jameson was starting to think the two were connected. He hadn't heard anything from his contact, who was supposed to track down her ex-boyfriend. Tomorrow, he'd have to follow up on that.

"If there's anything I can do . . ." she trailed off with a laugh when her stomach growled loudly.

It made him smile. "Do you want to get dinner?"

Her face lit up.

"As friends," he quickly added.

He could've sworn her eyes flashed with disappointment, but she agreed. "Sure."

* * * *

*Jameson*

They opted for Chinese takeout and enjoyed it back at Daisy's apartment—at her insistence. Jameson was flirting with trouble by being alone with her, but after the shots she'd taken from the few patrons at the restaurant, he'd agreed.

There was still so much mystery around her case that supposition kept the gossip lines hot, and the less she had to endure that, the better.

Over fried rice, they'd exchanged embarrassing stories featuring Dillon. Then they'd fought over dumplings as they'd reminisced about high school. Finally, they'd shared their fortunes as they got caught up on what each of them had done between then and now.

It had been easy to talk to her about all of it. A fact that surprised him. If he didn't have to constantly remind himself that they were just friends—whenever she flashed a smile at him, or she laughed, and the husky sound of it had excitement flooding through his veins—then he'd have no problem believing they could be.

They'd been talking for the better part of two hours when the conversation lagged. He stifled a yawn as the day started to catch up with him. "I should prob—"

"Oh! So, I ran into Shelly. That's some landlady you have, James." She hurriedly cut him off, and he struggled to catch up with her abrupt change in subject.

"Shelly? Yeah, I guess." Did Daisy like his landlady? He was confused as to why she would have brought the woman up.

Daisy smiled coyly. "She seems very fond of you."

He was sure he was missing something. Shelly may be fond of him, but the feeling wasn't mutual. These days, he avoided her as much as possible.

He rubbed at his forehead, but his tired brain was letting him down. "Is there a point to this?"

"You slept with her, didn't you?" She delivered the accusation with a snort of derision as she crossed her arms, all pretense of teasing gone.

His eyes went cold. Whatever enjoyment he'd been having in her company fled. Trying to be friends with Daisy was pointless if she was going to take any opportunity to swing at him. He ground his teeth as he thought about what had happened with Shelly.

It wasn't one of his prouder moments. He'd evaded Shelly's advances for months, but the night of the annual department barbecue—after Daisy had first come back to town—he'd had a few beers and . . . yeah. He'd had an itch, and Shelly had wanted to scratch it. It was a mistake. One he hadn't repeated since.

But what right did Daisy have to throw it in his face? He started to get hot as his temper rose to meet hers. "Oh, come off it, Daisy. You're judging me? Isn't the mess you're currently in because of who *you* slept with?" His voice was harsh, and his breathing had picked up speed to match it.

"What's that supposed to mean?" she yelled at him.

*Dammit!* He shouldn't have let his temper get the better of him. Now, he'd revealed something he wasn't ready for her to know.

"What haven't you told me?" She glared at him with her hands on her hips.

*Great job, idiot. Now you're going to have to tell her.* He closed his eyes and calmed himself down. When his breathing had steadied, he opened them.

She watched him, but the anger had left her gaze. Her eyes pinched in worry, and he hadn't even told her what they'd found.

"I've been trying to track Derrick down since your arrest. I talked to a contact in Chicago . . ." He paused and avoided her eyes, dreading what he had to say next. "They went to his home. There was blood and signs of a struggle."

She gasped, and the color drained from her face. "He's dead?"

Troubled by her shocked expression, he rushed on, "No. Well, we don't know." He lifted a hand to her shoulder and squeezed, wishing he could ease the worry she must be feeling. "I'm sorry. But, hey, the Chicago police will find him."

"What if he's hurt because of me?" When her eyes flooded with tears, it wrenched his heart.

"Hey, don't do that." He chucked her chin and pulled her into a hug.

Any anger he had at her wasn't important. Not when she was afraid like this. And he wouldn't let her feel guilty. Not because of something she had no control over.

"You don't know that. They could be framing you

because of him." And if they were, he would make sure everyone involved paid for it.

After several seconds, he felt her sigh. "I never found the key."

He pulled back to look at her face. "What?" He was having trouble keeping up with her line of thought.

"My spare key. I looked for it today, but I don't think he ever mailed it back." She'd stopped the tears from falling, but her eyelashes were wet.

His gaze shifted lower. He loved how tall Daisy was. It meant her lips were so close. At six foot four, he was used to bending in half to kiss a woman, but her lips were right there. Only inches away.

"Do you think someone could have taken it from him? To plant the drugs?"

He warned himself to focus on what she was saying, not how enticing her lips looked. After a mental shake, he digested what she'd said. "It's possible. You need to tell Blair about the key. It could help in court if this goes that far."

She flinched at the word 'court,' and Jameson cursed himself for bringing it up. He kissed her on the forehead and stepped back. "Don't worry about that now. I'm going to do everything I can to make sure it doesn't come to a trial."

She gave him a wan smile in return.

"You should get some rest." He started edging his way to the door, knowing he'd be tempted to stay if he didn't get out of there soon. If only as a friend—to offer her comfort.

*Yeah, right. As a friend.*

Daisy nodded, but before he could leave, she stopped him. He tensed, wondering if she was going to bring Shelly back up. "James, thank you. For tonight."

His muscles relaxed when she didn't, but when he met her gaze, it held so much longing that he tensed up again. Staring into her eyes, he almost caved and decided to stay.

Instead, he shot her a grin. "Catch you tomorrow." Then, he escaped before he had a chance to change his mind.

* * * *

*Chase*

Chase Sinclair was a businessman—a successful one at that. He had a reputation for making deals happen, no matter how reluctant a party might be. It was well-warranted. He knew how and when to apply pressure to get what he wanted. There'd only ever been one business proposition he'd failed to secure.

*Whiteford Farm.*

His hands clenched into fists, the ring he habitually wore biting into his palm, as he stared down at the model of a luxury golf community he'd never gotten to build—the one that should have gone up on Jake Redland's property.

The Redlands were supposed to have been an easy mark, but they'd had the audacity to try and get him thrown in prison. Of course, he'd immediately bought the judge and fixed that little issue. And the person who'd provided the misinformation had been punished. But that didn't ease his pride.

No, Chase Sinclair refused to lose. He'd find a way to get what he wanted . . . eventually. And if the Redland family suffered along the way, even better.

He'd already arranged for the sister to go to jail. There'd been a snag or two in his original plan, but he'd found a way to make it happen. The sergeant was a new concern but one he could handle if it became necessary. Poor cops died in the line of duty all the time, didn't they?

Chase circled the large meeting table where the model sat, waiting for the day he'd break ground on it.

And he would. He was confident the sergeant had nothing that tied him to the Redland case. He'd been very careful in that regard.

He fiddled with the ring on his right hand. It was an unconscious gesture that caused it to catch the light. He stared at it, admiring the symbol of a black rook set amid a bed of diamonds outlined in gold. It was flashy, yes. But it served a purpose.

One Emerson was well aware of.

He might have to sacrifice the judge but so be it. Chase wouldn't think twice if it was necessary to achieve his goals. Emerson was merely a pawn in the elaborate chess game he was playing.

And so was the woman. She'd face legal fees, especially if the case were long and drawn out. Those could be so draining. She might even have to sell her stake in the farm to make ends meet.

*Now, wouldn't that be a shame?* At the thought, his thin lips peeled back in a smile as vile as his heart.

# CHAPTER 14

*Daisy*

Daisy frowned at herself in the bathroom mirror. She'd been trying to create a smokey eye for the last hour, and she still wasn't happy with the results. How the girl in the video managed to do it in less than five minutes was beyond her.

With a sound of disgust, she tossed the eye shadow aside. So far, her seduction plan was off to a rocky start.

She'd already had to call in reinforcements when she realized she had nothing in her closet that said, "Undress me now." Thankfully, Blair was on her way over. She was fond of designer clothes and had jumped at the opportunity to turn Daisy into her personal Barbie doll.

At this rate, she would need Blair to do her makeup, too. But at least she'd been able to do something with her hair. She patted the waves she'd created and smiled. Her black locks were usually pin-straight, and she rarely bothered to style them any differently. But tonight was all about looking different, so she'd taken the time to curl it.

Jameson was doing too good a job of keeping her usual self at arm's length. They'd spent the rest of the week having dinner together in her apartment. He'd been dropping by after work and catching her up on any new information. Just like he would tonight. Though, so far, they hadn't found much.

Derrick was still missing, and she hoped he was all right. She didn't know if Jameson's hunch was correct and Derrick had gotten her mixed up in all this or if she was the culprit, but she held no grudge against her ex and didn't want to see him hurt.

Blair had been happy to hear about the key. If Derrick never returned it, they could use that fact to argue for her innocence if the case made it to trial, which looked more likely every day. They were no closer to finding The Rook or clearing her name.

The only good news had been when she'd finally gotten in touch with Dillon this morning. He and Lydia were coming home and would likely be here by Sunday. She couldn't wait to tell Jameson, knowing he'd been sweating the lack of communication with her brother.

But she'd tell him *after* she seduced him. There was no sense in bringing up Dillon and blowing any chance she had at making that happen.

She blew out a breath and braced her hands on either side of the sink. She could do this. She might be a relationship type of girl, but it's not like she didn't want that with him. The point of this was to get him to agree to build one with her. And he wasn't some stranger she'd picked up in a bar. She knew him. And she had to pull out all the stops if this was going to work.

Her experience, though it's not like she had a ton of it—but she *had* grown up with brothers—had taught her that men liked to stake claims. If Jameson wanted her, consciously or not, she was betting he'd laid one on her. All she had to do was make him think it was in jeopardy.

If only her stomach were as confident as her words. It felt like she'd swallowed a jar of butterflies. They were fluttering around in there and making her twitchy with nerves. She needed to get herself together before he showed up. Thankfully, she had a couple of hours until then.

Staring at herself, she gave one last thought to fixing the eye shadow before she gave up and wiped at it with a tissue, succeeding in smearing it down the side of her face. She howled in frustration just as a knock sounded on her door.

*Great timing.*

Leaving the smudge, she went to answer the door for Blair, opening the door with a scowl.

Her sister-in-law's eyes grew big, and then she chuckled. "Well, I can see I came at a good time."

Daisy laughed and ushered her inside. "Yes, I'm desperate. Please fix me."

Blair grinned. "I will, and then you get to try these." She held up a black dress bag and Daisy felt a hint of trepidation at what might be inside, but she smiled and shook it off.

She'd already made up her mind. This was happening.

"Can't wait. Let's hang those up in the bedroom." She

took the bag and went to hang it in her closet.

Back in the hall, Blair said, "Okay, let's see what I'm working with."

Daisy led Blair to the bathroom. What few cosmetics she had littered the counter.

Waving at them, she told her, "I can't get the smokey eye right. Whatever you think would look good. I'm giving you free rein."

Blair's eyes lit up, and she grinned. "I know just the thing!"

Daisy was happy that at least one of them was excited. She wasn't worried about what Blair might do. Her sister-in-law's face was always flawless, and it never looked gaudy. She envied Blair's ease with cosmetics. She was more comfortable with ponytails and cutoffs. Maybe it had been her height or that she'd only had brothers growing up, but Daisy had never mastered the art of makeup. That fact hadn't bothered her before, but she wanted tonight to be perfect.

After ten minutes of doing exactly as Blair directed, she was anxious to see the results. She'd closed her eyes, pursed her lips, stared at the heavens, and it had felt like a lot of things had been brushed on her face. She wasn't sure how all of it was going to turn out.

Her hands drummed on her legs in restless activity when Blair announced, "All done."

Daisy turned to look in the mirror. "Wow." Her mouth fell open. Blair had made her look like herself but an enhanced version. Her cheekbones were more prominent, her eyes were bigger, and her lips were darker, but it all looked natural.

Her sister-in-law squealed and clasped her hands together. "You like it?"

"I love it! If I knew how to do my makeup like this, I might wear it more often." She laughed, giddy with wonder. "Thank you."

Blair smiled and gave Daisy a quick hug. "You're welcome." She pulled back, her cheeks reddening as though she was slightly embarrassed.

The hug touched Daisy. She knew Blair was still reticent about showing affection, but they'd grown close over the last year. To each other, they were the sister they'd never had.

At least she'd had brothers and a loving family growing up. Blair had no siblings and a distant mother, whom Daisy had met only once at Jake and Blair's wedding, and the impression wasn't favorable.

Frowning over the memory, she reminded herself it didn't matter because Blair had a family now. "Okay, next order of business—the dress."

Blair squealed again and raced back to Daisy's bedroom. "I can't wait for you to see what I brought."

Her excitement was infectious. Daisy smiled, not having felt this light in days. She followed her sister-in-law, then took a seat on the bed while Blair unzipped the bag. She pulled out the first outfit and revealed it with a flourish.

Daisy chuckled at her enthusiasm and stared at the garment. It was a bright red dress. Struck by the color, she stood. Taking it from Blair, she held it up and inspected it further. There was a slit down the front, and the back draped in a deep "U" shape. It was a modest length, with one side reaching to the floor and the other stopping just above the knee. It looked amazing but also like something you'd wear to the Oscars.

"I think this might be a bit much."

Blair chewed her lip. "You're probably right. Here, what about this one." She reached back into the bag and produced a shiny gold tube dress.

Not only was it strapless, but Daisy could tell it wouldn't even cover her butt. She was at least half a foot taller than Blair, and most of it was leg. That tiny dress might be modest on her sister-in-law, but it would've been too revealing on her. She wanted to be tempting, but she didn't want to look like some bottom-shelf floozy.

"Um, I think that'll be too short on me."

Blair squinted at the dress, then at Daisy's legs. "Maybe."

Before she could insist Daisy try it on, she asked, "What else is in there?"

"I think this one is perfect for you." Blair pulled out a black dress and held it up.

It was sleeveless with a V-neck. There was ruching at the hips, and the length was probably to the knee on Blair, which meant it might not be too short for her.

Daisy smiled. "I like it."

Blair pushed it into her arms. "Try it on!"

She laughed and laid it on her bed while she shed her jeans and long-sleeve t-shirt.

When she'd changed into the dress, Blair pulled her over to stand in front of the full-length mirror by her dresser. "You look amazing!"

Daisy stared.

*Wow, this is a far cry from my usual look.*

She barely recognized herself. The dress was sexy but not slutty. It hugged her slim frame and made her look like she had hips. The "V" showed off just enough cleavage, and with the dress hitting a little above mid-thigh, she looked . . . hot.

She hoped Jameson thought so, too.

Staring at her reflection, the reality of what she was doing hit her, and her stomach dropped. "Is this crazy? It's a crazy idea, isn't it? Maybe I should just forget the whole thing."

Blair turned her around and gave her hands a squeeze. "I'm hardly an expert on relationships, but you both deserve to think about something other than your case for a bit. So," she paused, and a grin spread across her face, "if you want him, why not go get him?"

Daisy nodded. She did want him. And he wanted her; he'd told her as much. They could be together already if he weren't hung up on her being Dillon's sister. Tonight, she was determined to make him forget that. And, shoot, if she was going to prison, she didn't want to miss out on what little time she had left with him.

Daisy nodded. "I'm going to get him."

* * * *

*Jameson*

Despite his lack of progress on Daisy's case, Jameson was

eager to see her. Finishing work and driving to her quadplex was the best part of his day. They'd gotten into a routine, and it suited him.

He'd drop by after work and catch her up on any new information he'd found. Then they'd get dinner and spend it talking about anything *but* the case.

The deadline to prove her innocence was looming, but she didn't let that cripple her. She was strong, and he admired the hell out of her for it.

Grinning at the mere prospect of seeing her sunny face, he climbed the steps to her apartment. He felt warm, but it wasn't because the temperature had finally risen above fifty. No, this warmth came from the inside. He and Daisy had become friends.

He was proud of himself for learning to be comfortable in her presence.

Sure, he might have to corral his thoughts on occasion. Still, for the most part, he'd become successful at picturing her solely as his friend—like Dillon, who was never allowed to go on vacation again.

He was pretty sure his lack of progress on Daisy's case had a lot to do with his lack of pull in the department. The captain hadn't sanctioned any part of the investigation he'd conducted on her behalf. It was a problem for the courts, according to their asshole of a captain. Jameson had other duties to focus on, like calming down Ms. Simmons after the neighbor's dog killed her boxwoods.

*Potential drug trafficking was less important.* He grimaced at the memory.

He'd tried and failed to point that out to the captain.

The man was as biased as they came, and he was looking forward to the day the captain either got promoted out of Rolling Brook or retired. The man had refused to acknowledge that finding such a large cache of drugs tied to a distributor in Chicago was something worth looking into. Their job was to keep Rolling Brook safe, and that sure as hell felt like a threat to Jameson.

He shook his head. Well, he didn't need the captain's permission. He was looking into it anyway—for Daisy.

Smiling again at the thought of her, he knocked on her door.

When she opened it, his smile died, his mouth fell open, and he almost swallowed his tongue.

"Hi, James." Her grin had a hint of the wicked as she stood, hip cocked to the side, in a little black dress.

He couldn't think, much less form words. His thoughts fled south along with his blood, so he merely stood and stared.

She chuckled, and the sound washed over him, causing his body to stir. "Want to come in?"

He thought he nodded, and she turned away. He followed her, almost in a trance, as he watched her hips sway against the ruched material of the dress.

She settled on the couch and crossed her legs, causing the short dress to ride up even further. She had such gorgeous long legs.

He sat across from her, forgetting his rule about staying off the too-cozy couch, then looked her up and down.

*What is she wearing?*

And her face, it was painted. He rarely saw it that way.

*Did I know her cheekbones could look like that?*

And her eyes. Were they even more blue? He'd never seen her so made up and dressed so . . . so sexy.

*Man, she was sexy.*

She leaned toward him, bracing one hand on the cushion that separated them. The "V" of the neckline gaped, and his gaze caught on her breasts.

"How did it go today?"

At her question, he blinked. His brain felt fuzzy, and his pants were too tight. He focused on her face and tried to form a coherent thought.

Her eyes were big and wide, and he thought he could drown in their blue depths. "Any new leads?"

*Leads?* He'd like to lead her somewhere, all right. Her scent drifted over him, and he breathed deep, savoring the musky aroma. She was spicy like cinnamon and earthy like flowers. The combination was a heady one that he couldn't get enough of.

"On the case?" A smile teased her lips as he only stared, transfixed.

*A case?* He was imagining licking her everywhere her scent lingered when her words finally penetrated.

*Shit! The case.* The reason he was here.

*Dammit, James, rein it in. Whatever this is, the answer is still no. You can't have her.*

He leaned away from her and that tempting smell. Then he urged his brain to clear and give her an answer. But it stalled.

Wait, why was she dressed like that? Was she going somewhere?

His chest ached when he realized their routine wouldn't happen tonight. He'd been looking forward to spending the evening with her.

He cleared his throat over the lump that had just formed in it. "No, not really. Um, Daisy?"

"Yes?" She was still leaning toward him, but he forced himself to keep his eyes on her face.

"Were you going somewhere?" His tone was flat, but he kept his expression neutral.

She didn't answer him, and his stomach dropped. He looked into her eyes, but they were hooded. Like she was hiding something, she didn't want to tell him.

*No, no fucking way.*

"Do you have a date?" he asked through clenched teeth.

She made a noncommittal noise and rose. He was right behind her. He shot off the couch and grabbed her arm before she'd taken more than a step.

"Who is he?" he growled, his face flushing in anger.

"Why do you care?" She taunted, and his control snapped.

*How can she go on a date with someone just like that? So, what? The last week meant nothing to her?*

She thought she could toss him aside and spend the night with whatever yahoo came sniffing around. Damned if he'd let her.

He bared his teeth as he fantasized, pulverizing whoever she thought she was going out with into the ground. No, she wasn't going anywhere. Not if he had anything to say about it.

"No." His eyes turned cold as steel as he delivered his

decree.

"No, what? You don't get a say in who I choose to go out with, James." She tugged at her arm, but he held it firm.

"The hell I don't."

Her eyes sparkled in victory, but all Jameson saw was red. He yanked her to him and crushed his lips to hers, intent on staking his claim.

He felt possessed as he devoured her mouth. His desire for her was an animal, starved beyond measure. It clawed at him as he drank her in, ravenous for her taste. His hands raced over her, groping, marking, absorbed with showing her she was *his*.

He'd wanted her for too long to let someone else have her. She would be his. And *only* his, consequences be damned.

# CHAPTER 15

*Daisy*

Holy cow, her ploy worked! Daisy's head reeled as much from her success as the sensations flooding her. She'd finally gotten Jameson to kiss her, and, oh boy, was he kissing her. It was like the first time but more intense. The urgency was there, but it played second fiddle to the hunger with which he tasted her. And his hands. They roamed her body, causing her skin to tingle everywhere he touched. It was enough to drive her crazy with need.

When she thought she couldn't stand it any longer, he broke the kiss and cupped her face in his hands. His eyes were so fierce. It stirred something primal in her belly. A desire to claim him as he'd claimed her.

"You're mine." His words sent a shiver through her, but it wasn't fear.

Joy bloomed in her chest and left her breathless so that she could only nod.

Jameson shook his head. "Say it," he demanded, his

voice gruff with his struggle for control.

She sucked in a breath, caught in his gaze, her head held captive in his strong hands. She'd never seen him like this, and it was exciting. Her pulse raced as she lifted her arms to cup his face. "You're mine."

He grinned at that, but it was wicked as his eyes stayed sharp on hers. She was fully aware that's not what he'd meant for her to say. But if she was going to be his, he had to be hers too.

He released her face and caressed her back on the way to her bottom. When he grabbed her seat and pressed his arousal against her, she gasped at the intimate contact, and her thighs clenched. Once the shock had worn off, she wrapped one of her legs around his and arched into him, unwilling to break the contact.

"Is that what you want, Daisy?" His voice whispered in her ear and sent delicious little shivers all the way to her toes.

*Boy, did she.*

Words were getting muddled in her brain, but she thought she moaned the word "Yes" when he placed open-mouthed kisses on her exposed neck.

Her skin pebbled under his attention. He was teasing her, and she liked it. She liked it a lot. If he was a drug, she could easily become addicted.

But she'd always been one to give as good as she got. "James?"

His teasing kisses had moved lower, and his answer was muffled against her chest when he murmured, "Yeah?"

She clenched her hands in his uniform shirt as he

clamped his mouth around her breast through the fabric of the dress.

"You're wearing too many clothes," she wheezed between breaths.

It was her turn to tease, and she wanted—needed—him bare. Her palms ached with the desire to touch his skin. To have all those yummy muscles under her hands.

"Am I?" He nibbled on her, causing warmth to pool between her thighs.

*Oh my.* It had been too long, and she wanted this man too much. She could already feel the pressure building. It was a ball of heat radiating through her.

"Yes, I want . . ." Her mind went blank when he trailed his fingers up her inner thigh.

Her desire had turned into a fever that was leaving delirium in its path. He groaned and fused his mouth to hers again when he found she wasn't wearing anything under the dress.

Their tongues tangled and sparred as both tried to assert their will over the other. Each thrust of his tongue she parried with one of her own until Jameson plunged his fingers inside her.

With his hand, he began to mimic the movement of his tongue, and she surrendered, moaning into his mouth as more heat blossomed inside of her. It opened her up like the flower she was named after.

His hand cupped her, and her whole body flushed. It was too hot. The fever burned her like the sun scorched the earth. Her petals would wilt under its rays. She panted against the onslaught, but he didn't let up.

He pulled back to look into her face. "Come for me, Daisy," he rasped out.

His pupils had grown, and she stared—locked in their dark depths as he stroked her. They flashed with blue fire and scorched her body and soul. The flames were relentless; she had no choice but to obey. Pleasure swamped her, and she cried out. When her legs gave out from under her, he held her up.

Light-headed in the aftermath, she dropped her head against his shoulder.

*Whoa.*

That had staggered her. With her nose buried in his chest, his scent washed over her—black coffee and oak. It was masculine and all Jameson. She could still feel his arousal pressing into her stomach, but she needed a moment to get her bearings. She felt as high as she would've been if she'd used the cocaine they'd found in her apartment.

But he didn't give her a chance to come back down. Her breathing hadn't even slowed when he grabbed her legs and hiked them around his waist.

"My turn."

He walked them backward and laid her on the kitchen table. She gasped as the cold wood met the exposed skin of her back.

Sitting up, she unbuttoned his shirt while he undid the holster at his waist. It made a loud thunk when it landed, making her glad she was on the first floor.

She freed him from the uniform shirt, then huffed in annoyance at the white undershirt that still hid his chest from her. Desperate to have it off him, she reached into his pants and grinned at his jump. He hissed out a breath and nipped at her neck.

Laughing, she tugged the shirt loose, and he helped her pull it over his head.

*He's so beautiful.*

She loved how broad his shoulders were, like some Scottish warrior from a romance novel cover. They made her, the giant of a woman she was, feel small.

She trailed her fingers over his abs, across his pecs, then she pulled him closer by wrapping her legs around his waist and did the thing she'd been wanting to do for days.

Sinking her teeth into the muscles of his shoulder, she tasted him. He was salty from sweat.

When he groaned, pleasure shot to her center. She felt powerful, knowing she could make him as weak as he'd made her.

Drunk on the knowledge, she licked and nipped her way up to his ear. "You're still wearing too many clothes."

"So are you." He tugged at the dress, and she had a moment of panic when she thought he'd been about to rip it off her.

She had no idea how much Blair paid for it, but she knew it was more than she could afford. But he only ran his hands up her thighs, shoving the dress out of the way as he gripped her hips.

Watching him and the hunger in his eyes, she leaned back and slipped the dress straps off her shoulders. She was a little self-conscious, knowing he usually went for the busty type, but his response had her fears evaporating.

With a hum of pleasure, he cupped her bare breasts in his palms. She was enjoying his hands on her, but she wanted to see him.

She pointed at his trousers. "Your turn."

His eyes burned with the heat of his craving for her, and she gulped when he kept her stare while he undid the zipper and shed the rest of his clothes.

On a blink, her gaze landed lower. *Oh, oh my.*

She'd felt him, but Jameson was a big man in every possible way. When she reached for him, he stayed her hand, placing it over her head as he laid her back on the table. The cold had her gasping again, but she quickly forgot it as his mouth closed over her breast.

Holding her captive, he feasted on her until she writhed beneath him. The fever raced through her, burning her from the inside out.

When he released her hands, she ran them over him, desperate to touch him and make him as ravenous as she was. Their eyes locked as he gripped her hips. She held her breath as he entered her, then released it with a moan as he filled her so completely.

She stretched around him, her nails digging into his arms as he began to move. He started slow, but it wasn't enough. The heat raged through her, and she wanted more.

She reared up and wrapped her arms around his neck. "More!" she commanded, and together, they set a pace that had both their hearts thudding against their chests.

Her bottom slapped against the cold table as she moved with him, but she didn't care. A merciless hunger for pleasure had overtaken her, and she was helpless to do anything but feed it.

She had her hands in his red curls, and when she felt the pressure boil over, she locked eyes with him. He was close; she knew he was.

Unable to stop it, her head fell back on a scream as the climax seared through her. He cursed, and on a shudder, hurtled after her.

Spent, they collapsed onto the table, chests pumping from the exertion. She felt like she was floating, drugged with pleasure, and high on the knowledge that this would change things between them. Finally, Jameson would see they were too good together not to try and make it work, Dillon or not.

Slowly, she came back to her surroundings. Her body was still connected to his, and she wrapped her arms around him, beaming with glee. The table was hard and cold on her back, but she didn't mind. She was too euphoric to let that intrude on her happiness. There was a warmth in her chest, but it was from more than merely the contact with his. It might be winter outside, but it was spring in her heart.

He grunted and pushed himself up on his forearms, hovering over her with that wicked grin on his face. "Right about now, your date's probably getting pretty pissed that you stood him up."

She chuckled and traced his grin with a finger. "James, the only date I had was with you."

His grin disappeared, and he shoved his way to his feet. "What?"

*Uh-oh.*

That's not the reaction she'd been expecting. She shivered and sat up. The heat of his body was gone, and his eyes had turned equally cold.

She crossed her arms over herself, worried he would be angry with her. She'd thought they could laugh about her seducing him, but she had to tread carefully if that was going to happen.

# CHAPTER 16

*Jameson*

*What the fuck? Did she mean . . .?*

Jameson stumbled away from Daisy, his hands clenching into fists. She'd lied to him. The picture was suddenly, pathetically, clear. The hair, the face, the dress was all just a trick, and he'd fallen for it like some love-struck idiot.

Daisy slipped the straps of the dress back over her shoulders and hopped off the table. Coming to stand in front of him, she reached out a hand, but he flinched and turned away. He couldn't handle her touching him right now.

"There's no one else." Her words were delivered carefully, but each one hit him like a jab to the chest.

He'd broken the rules, been ready to forget the reasons they shouldn't be together, and it was all based on a lie.

The anger brewing inside him made his voice clipped when he replied, "Yeah, I'm getting that."

She had to know he was upset with her, but there was a smile in her voice when she teased, "I thought you'd be happy about that." Out of the corner of his eye, he saw her wave a hand at herself. "This was all for you, James. For *us*."

*For them?*

He turned and speared her with a look as cold as ice. "There wasn't supposed to be an *us*."

She winced, and he would've felt bad for saying it. But resentment was taking precedence.

"But there could be. James—" She reached for his arm again, but he shrugged her off.

Ignoring her, he walked to his clothes and started to get dressed.

"I've got two weeks before prison is a very likely possibility. Do you really want to spend the rest of that time mad at me?"

She was trying to reason with him, but he wasn't in the mood to hear it. She'd betrayed his trust. Whatever her reasons, he wasn't sure he could forgive her for that.

He fastened his belt and forced himself to look at her. The fact she was even hotter mussed from sex made his face flush in fury. "You're not going to prison."

He may be pissed at her, but there was no way he was letting that happen. Not for something she didn't do.

She huffed out a breath and propped her hands on her hips. "You can't guarantee that."

"I appreciate the vote of confidence." His lips curled down in a sneer.

*What kind of relationship could they have if she didn't*

*even trust me to clear her name?*

"You know I didn't mean it like that." Her tone was accusatory as if he was in the wrong here. "I've seen it with Dillon. I know how hard solving a case can be, and we're up against a short deadline."

*Dillon. His best friend.* The whole reason he was supposed to be staying miles away from Daisy. He'd fucked up majorly, and he was going to have to tell her brother.

He sighed; the fight went out of him. "I have to go."

"Wait! You can't leave like this." Her voice shook with desperation as she hurried after him on his way to the door.

He paused with a hand on the knob, but he couldn't turn around, unable to look at her. "Daisy, you manipulated me."

Behind him, he heard her gasp softly. "No, I—"

He glanced at her over his shoulder. "You did. I'd expect that from another woman but not from you. I thought you were better than that."

She'd known his reasons for wanting to keep things platonic between them, and she'd gone and trounced all over them anyway.

Her mouth dropped open, and the color drained from her face. Turning away, he opened the door and left her shocked and shaken. The same way he was feeling.

* * * *

*Daisy*

Daisy stared at her front door, a blank look in her eyes.

Her stomach churned along with her thoughts as she tried to process what just happened.

*"You're mine."* She could still hear Jameson saying the words, and yet he'd just closed the door in her face.

How had everything gone from blissfully perfect to completely messed up? She felt nauseated and swallowed against the sensation.

Because he was twisting things around.

She shook her head and started to pace. She hadn't manipulated him. She'd only wanted him to see that they could make it work between them. But, oh, the tone of his voice when he'd said that had cut her deeply. She rubbed at her chest as if it would ease the ache there. He'd been so disappointed he couldn't look at her, and it had caused her stomach to roil in shame.

Clutching at it, she collapsed on the couch. She'd made a huge mess of things. She'd been so focused on making Jameson see the possibility of them as a couple that she hadn't thought about the fact that he might not want a relationship with her. He'd done exactly what she'd been worried about.

He'd loved her and left her.

Her breath caught on a sob as that reality hit her. He chose to place the blame on her because she wasn't what he wanted anyway. At least not for the long term.

*Did he even do relationships?*

She'd gone and given him the one thing he *did* want—sex. No wonder he walked away.

*Good job, Daisy.*

The tears broke free and streamed down her cheeks,

making tracks in her carefully made-up face. Not caring, she curled into a ball and buried her face in a pillow. Her mind replayed every minute of the last week with him, and it was agony. She thought she'd gotten to know him again, but she'd been stupid, seeing only what she wanted to see.

She cried for the schoolgirl who'd had a crush on the boy and the silly woman who'd grown to love the man. Neither had wanted her.

She should've known; zebras can't change their stripes.

* * * *

*Daisy*

By Monday, Daisy headed back to work. Dillon and Lydia had gotten home late on Sunday, but she hadn't had the energy to talk to them. After everything that had happened with Jameson, she hadn't had the chance to tell him Dillon was on his way back. But keeping him updated wasn't on her list of priorities anymore. Anything dealing with her case she'd discuss with her brother from now on.

As far as Daisy was concerned, she and Jameson had no more reason to cross paths. She didn't need the reminder of everything she'd wanted and couldn't have. He'd thrown any chance at that away when he'd tossed her aside like some woman he'd picked up for a one-night stand.

When she got to the diner, Shug took one look at her and sent her home. Daisy didn't blame her. Her reflection told her she looked like H-E-Double Hockey Sticks.

She stared at herself in her bathroom mirror and

sighed. Dark circles colored the skin under her eyes, and she managed to look haggard like she'd lost a few pounds she didn't have to lose. Food hadn't exactly been on her mind a lot this past weekend.

The whole thing was a bit hazy. She thought she'd spent most of it in a heap on the couch, nursing the wounds Jameson had inflicted.

Because she'd been stupid enough to fall in love with him.

In truth, she didn't think she'd ever stopped loving him. He'd always had a little piece of her heart, and at the first opportunity, she'd given the rest of it to him.

*Foolish.*

She shook her head. She'd been foolish, and that made it hurt all the worse. She was smarter than that. Or at least, she'd thought she was.

She'd had other relationships and loved other men. But none of them had ever had her whole heart. The little piece of it that belonged to Jameson had always been kept locked away, waiting for the day he'd finally want it.

She snorted at her stupidity and frowned. Clearly, that was never going to happen. It was time for her to pick up the pieces and move on.

She rummaged through her makeup bag, looking for a concealer to at least fix her face. The rest would heal in time . . . she hoped. Finding the cream, Daisy went to work on the circles under her eyes, knowing if she showed up at Lydia and Dillon's looking like she did, they'd be talking about a lot more than her case.

She wasn't ready for that—not yet.

# CHAPTER 17

*Jameson*

Jameson hunched over the computer as he combed through the National Crime Information Center database, looking for any connections to The Rook. The scowl on his face was the same one he'd been wearing all week. Other officers in the station had no idea what had changed the usually jovial Sergeant Jameson into the sullen creature he was now, but they'd learned to leave him alone. It was Wednesday, and he'd gotten no closer to solving Daisy's case.

The woman was driving him crazy even in her absence. He hadn't thought of much else over the last few days.

He'd hurt her. The look on her face when he'd left haunted his dreams . . . but she'd hurt him, too.

He hadn't had a relationship with a woman in years. Hookups, sure, but no one that he cared about, not since the barbeque. He'd saved that part of himself for Daisy, even knowing she was unattainable. But all they seemed good at together was fighting.

*Well . . . and fucking.*

Sex with her had been intense. He hadn't been gentle even though he was used to being careful with women because they were always so much smaller, but not Daisy. With her, he hadn't needed to worry about that.

She hadn't balked and run away screaming. She'd taken it and given it right back to him. It had been hot, fast, hard.

*And it was amazing.*

He'd crashed on top of her, smashing her into the table because his brain cells had leaked out along with his strength. He was no stranger to release, but that had been unlike anything he'd ever experienced.

*Doesn't matter because there's zero chance of it happening again.*

His scowl deepened at the thought. He was pretty sure leaving the way he did had won him a prominent spot on the list of people she hated.

Not that he was thrilled with her at the moment, but he knew her, and she wasn't likely to let that go. Maybe she'd tricked him, but he'd basically called her a harlot to her face.

And he still had to tell Dillon. He'd talked to him over the phone, but that was something better said in person, maybe over a beer or two—or six. Plus, they'd had more important things to discuss, like tracking down whoever was framing his sister.

Man, he had a headache. Jameson scrunched his eyes closed and dropped his head in his hands. Dillon was working from home since he was technically on vacation, so he'd continued to use the lieutenant's office. It was nice to have some separation from the bullpen when he didn't want to talk to anyone.

He'd resorted to massaging his temples to try and ease the tension when the phone rang and made him jump. "Dammit!"

With a murderous expression on his face, he picked up the receiver. "Jameson," he barked.

"We found your suspect." The voice on the other end of the line was all business. It was Detective Alonso of the Chicago P.D., Jameson's contact in the city. They'd gone to the police academy together and kept in touch for situations like these.

*Finally, a break in the case!*

He sat up straighter and gripped the phone as his adrenaline soared. "Where is he?"

"The morgue."

"Fuck!" It was hard to question a dead man. Why could no part of helping Daisy be easy?

"Yeah, sorry, man. I know that's not the news you were looking for." The detective's voice softened as he commiserated.

"Do you know what happened?" Scenarios started to race through his brain. Maybe it was connected to Daisy somehow, and it wouldn't all be a loss. He needed a lead, dammit.

"Not yet. We had a John Doe wash up in the river last week. Examiner ID'd him this morning as Derrick Thompson. Said it's foul play, so your suspect is now my murder victim."

If Daisy's ex was killed around the same time the drugs showed up in her apartment, the two had to be connected.

*Ah, fuck.* He was going to have to tell her that Derrick was dead.

"Hey, Alonso? Keep me in the loop. There's no way this isn't related to my case."

"Yeah, I was thinking the same. Share and share alike, my friend." There was a smile in the detective's voice now.

"You bet. But you just killed the only lead I had." His scowl relaxed as he joked with his friend. At least he had new information on her case and a chance at finding more.

The detective chuckled. "Maybe his corpse will tell us something. His dwelling's been ruled a crime scene, so I'll also take another look at that. I'll let you know whatever I find."

"Thanks, man. I owe you one." He felt some of the tension leave his head as he thought about this new development.

"I'll add it to your tab." Detective Alonso disconnected, and Jameson hung up the receiver.

He stared absently at the wall across from the desk as he ran through everything he knew about Daisy's ex-boyfriend.

Thompson had been a realtor in Chicago who liked to buy properties and turn them into rentals. The man had done very well for himself as far as Jameson could tell, but were the luxury cars and apartments, the hefty amount of investment properties, all acquired legally, or had he been mixed up in something shady enough to get him killed?

He was leaning towards the latter option. But what type of dealings? Had it been drugs? Could he be tied to The Rook? Would he have been able to hide that from Daisy? Or had he only recently gotten tangled up with whoever that bastard was?

Maybe Daisy could help fill in some of the blanks because he had too many questions and not enough answers right now.

Still, he wasn't looking forward to delivering this piece of news, even if it did give him an excuse to see her again.

Glancing at the clock on the computer screen, he thought she'd be at work, so he'd drop by later. Hopefully, she wouldn't slam the door in his face. At least not until after he questioned her about Thompson.

The scowl had returned to Jameson's face as he made himself go back to the criminal database, forcing thoughts of Daisy from his mind.

* * * *

*Daisy*

When she heard the knock at her door, Daisy thought about ignoring it. She'd collapsed onto her bed without plans to move before morning. She was so tired of pretending everything was okay, that all the questions about her arrest didn't bother her, that her heart wasn't still a weeping wound.

Somehow, she'd gotten through her shift at the diner the last two days with a sunny smile on her face, but she didn't have the energy to muster one now.

The knock sounded louder this time, and she sighed long and low. Making herself crawl out of bed, she forced one foot in front of the other with concerted effort until she stood at her front door.

"Daisy, open up. It's important." Jameson's voice bellowed out at her, and she flinched.

It was too soon. She didn't want to see him.

"I saw your car. I know you're here." He practically shouted at her, making her want to open the door, if only to slam it in his face.

*Will he go away if I ignore him?*

When she didn't respond, his voice gentled. "Look, I know you don't want to see me, but this is about Derrick. Please let me in."

*Derrick?*

Maybe they'd found him. Knowing she had little choice, Daisy finally opened the door. The small consolation was that she didn't have to smile for him.

He looked a little rough around the edges, so perhaps she hadn't been the only one suffering. He had faint purple smudges under his eyes, and the red curls on top of his head were a mess, as if he'd run his hands through them and pulled.

Her fingers itched to comb them into place. But she couldn't—wouldn't—touch him.

"What about Derrick?" She challenged as she blocked the door, one hand held at the ready to shut it in his face, the other propped on her hip.

"Can I come in?" he wheedled.

Oh, he'd like that, wouldn't he? Well, she wasn't going

to let him. There were too many memories of the last time he'd been inside her apartment that she was still trying to exorcise.

She was about to refuse him when he said, "You don't want me to do this out here." His eyes had softened, and they made tears burn behind her eyelids.

Her face fell, but she blinked them back. It was that bad, then. She stepped aside, deflated, and let Jameson enter.

He started toward her kitchen table, paused, blushed, and reversed course to sit on her couch. She would've chuckled at his embarrassment if the action hadn't stabbed at her wounds. As it was, it only caused her more pain.

She swallowed hard to clear the tightness in her throat, took a deep breath, and followed him to the sofa.

After several uncomfortable seconds, it was clear he didn't know where to start.

She wanted him out and this over with as soon as possible, so she broke the silence. "They found him?"

He lifted his hand to grasp hers, but she moved away from him. She wouldn't let him touch her, not when it didn't mean the same thing to him as it did to her.

"He's dead, Daisy. I'm sorry." His voice was gruff and cut as much as the clipped words.

She sucked in a breath and squeezed her eyes shut. She'd expected, but it was still a bit of a shock. "What happened?" She opened her lids and got caught in his somber gaze.

His mouth twisted into a grim line. "That's what we're

going to figure out, but there was evidence of foul play."

She went stiff as the implications fell over her. "Someone killed him?" Why would someone have done that? What had he gotten mixed up in?

Jameson nodded. "Do you know if he had any enemies? Or even colleagues who were competitive? Anyone that would have wanted to do him harm?"

Did she? She didn't think so. She hadn't seen Derrick in almost a year. Surely, there was someone else who could answer those questions.

"No, no one comes to mind. But James, I hadn't seen him in so long. Wouldn't someone else—closer to him—be a better source for those answers?"

"Probably. The Chicago police will handle that. But you're here, and something tells me this is tied to your case."

He scrubbed a hand over his face, and she noticed his stubble. It looked longer than usual as if he hadn't shaved this morning. She wondered what it would feel like. Especially right there on the cleft in his chin.

Realizing she was staring, she mentally scolded herself and focused on what he'd said. "Why do you think it's connected to me?"

He shrugged. "A gut feeling? The two events occurred close together, and I don't believe in coincidence."

"Okay, so what do we, er, I do next?" She had to remind herself that she was working on this with Dillon now. Jameson was only the messenger. One she wouldn't need to talk to after today.

*But maybe I need to make that clear.*

He frowned at her use of 'I.' "Let me know if you think of anyone that might have been a threat to Derrick, anything that you remember that seemed out of the norm or strange meetings, anything at all that didn't feel right. Call me."

*No.* She wouldn't. Daisy fixed him with her stare as she said, "I'll let Dillon know if I think of anything. I'm sure he'll keep you informed."

His eyes sparked at that. "Fine. Great."

He rose, but she stayed where she was; he could see himself out.

When the door slammed behind him, she let the tears fall. They weren't for Jameson. She was done crying over him.

No, she cried for Derrick. For a man she'd spent nearly two years of her life with, whom she'd cared for, who hadn't deserved to die in such a way.

# CHAPTER 18

*Jameson*

Rock music blared overhead, and the air was thick with the stench of unwashed gym socks. It was Saturday at the rec center, and the boxing room was packed. People milled about; several of them hovered at the edge of the ring, ready to claim it as soon as the current occupants vacated.

Jameson was oblivious to the smell and the noise, and he didn't notice the crowd as he and Dillon circled one another. They'd been going at it for twenty minutes, and sweat covered both—one dark, the other light. Both were tall, but he had a few inches and several pounds on his friend.

When Dillon took a swing at him, Jameson dodged and countered with a punch of his own that the lieutenant easily blocked.

"What's with you? Daisy hits harder than that," Dillon taunted. He swiped at his brow and grinned, his blue eyes so like his twin's.

Jameson flinched at the mention of her. He'd been absorbed with how to broach the topic of him and Daisy to her brother for the entirety of their match. His heart wasn't in the fight, and he'd barely done more than parry and block Dillon's blows.

"She probably does," he muttered, then weaved away from Dillon's rear hook.

He was sure if given the chance, Daisy would like to take a swing at him. How she reacted when he'd seen her last made that clear.

He'd told her about her ex in person because he'd known it would hurt her, and he'd wanted to be there for her. But she'd pushed away any comfort he'd offered. It stung. Especially when she was the one who'd wronged *him*.

He wasn't so pissed at her that he hadn't tried to help ease the blow, but she'd brushed him off like he'd meant nothing, like the sex hadn't been incredible, and she had no desire to repeat the experience.

Well, dammit, that wasn't fair. She could've at least apolo—

Dillon's lead cross dropped Jameson to his knees. Pain exploded inside his head, and he saw stars. He'd been lost in his thoughts and hadn't blocked the punch.

"Shit! James, are you okay?" Dillon knelt beside him while he gingerly felt his nose—a task that proved difficult with gloves on.

He didn't think it was broken, but it sure as hell hurt badly enough. His face felt like it was on fire, and the blaze centered there.

"Yeah, nice shot." He tried to smile, but it turned into a grimace when the movement had the fire burning across his face. Trying to hide it, he stood up and regained his stance.

Dillon looked him over and shook his head. "I think we're done for today."

"You only want to stop because you think you beat me for once," Jameson goaded, but it was half-hearted. He was ready for the match to be over, even if he was the loser.

"Maybe." Dillon grinned and waved at the boxers who were hovering. "But let's give these guys a turn, yeah?"

He nodded. Relief had caused his mouth to go dry. That or it was from dread because he still had to tell Dillon about sleeping with his sister.

Jameson swallowed and cleared his throat as he joined his friend on the bench beside the ring. They'd left their bags there, and he stripped off his gloves, tossing them inside. Grabbing his water bottle, he took a big swig.

"Okay, sergeant, spill. Your head's been somewhere else all morning. What's going on?" Dillon's voice rang with the authoritative tone of a lieutenant speaking to his junior officer.

It had Jameson cursing under his breath, knowing he had to answer. "If I tell you, you're probably going to want to punch me again." He carefully probed his nose.

Not broken, but still very hot.

Dillon's eyes were shrewd as he assessed his friend. "You finally made a move on Daisy."

"What?" Jameson whipped his head around so fast it nearly shook his brain. "How'd you . . .?"

The lieutenant shrugged. "Lydia."

That made sense. Lydia was a therapist, and they tended to see things others tried to hide.

"And you're not mad?" He tensed, ready for Dillon to lay into him.

But his friend chuckled. "That punch hit you harder than I thought if you think I have any say over Daisy and who she dates."

Jameson frowned in confusion. That wasn't the answer he'd been expecting. He felt like he'd sparred against an opponent only to discover he'd been fighting himself.

Then Dillon's expression sobered. "I love you like a brother, but if you hurt her . . . I'll get Jake involved, and we'll both kick your ass."

He winced. "Yeah, I think I already did that."

"Do I want to know what happened?"

*She seduced me, and we had sex on her kitchen table.*

"Probably not." Some things were better left unsaid.

"Are you going to fix it, or do I need to call Jake?"

"I want to fix it." And not just because he didn't want the Redland brothers beating the shit out of him. He missed Daisy—seeing her smiling face after work every day, talking to her about anything and everything, and kissing her sweet plum lips.

"Then don't be an idiot. Go patch things up with her." Dillon slapped him on the back and stood, signaling the end of the conversation.

*Right, patch things up.*

He could do that . . . couldn't he?

*** * * ***

*Jameson*

By Monday morning, Jameson had come up with a plan. He'd spent the rest of the weekend thinking about what had happened between him and Daisy. Most of it had been agonizing over her reasons for seducing him.

What had been her motive?

Did she have one?

Or did she simply want to be with him?

He'd puzzled over it for hours, even compared her actions to those of other women he'd been with until he finally realized the comparison wasn't fair.

What he had with Daisy was different.

In a short span of time, they'd become close, plus they had a shared childhood—shared memories. He knew her better than he'd known any woman.

And knowing her, he'd realized that she'd seduced him because she wanted to be with him. Nothing more—no ulterior reasons.

When he thought about it that way, the fact she'd wanted him enough to seduce him in the first place was flattering.

So, he planned to be the bigger person and apologize. What was a little groveling if it meant she forgave him? Besides, her seducing him had been hot. And he'd like her to do it again. And again. And again.

Grinning like an idiot, he picked up the station phone as it rang. "Jameson."

"In a good mood already? If you hadn't been, this

would've done the trick," Detective Alonso baited.

Jameson sat up straighter as excitement spiked in his veins. "What have you found?"

"A hidden camera. Want to know what was on it?"

"Fucker. You know I do." His pulse picked up speed as he waited for the answer.

Alonso's laugh reverberated through the receiver. "Seems our pal Thompson invested in it as a security policy. Too bad it didn't save his life."

"And? What did it capture?" He was running out of patience for Alonso's stalling.

"All business today, I see," when he paused, Jameson wanted to reach through the phone and shake his friend. "One prominent Mr. Chase Sinclair, a couple of suits, and Mr. Thompson having quite the argument over a woman."

"Daisy Redland?" Jameson held his breath.

"Ding, ding, ding. What do we have for him, folks?"

He let it out in a rush. "Fuck, Alonso. What did they say?"

"I guess Thompson owed Sinclair a favor, and he tried to call it in. Wanted him to hide part of their shipment in her apartment. Thompson refused, and that got him smacked around a little. Eventually, he caved and handed over a key. After that, the suits dragged him from the room."

He processed all that and shot to his feet. "I need a copy." The video would be enough to prove Daisy's innocence—to show she was set up.

"I figured. But, hey, I didn't even tell you the best part."

"What else was on there?" His mind raced. He had to

tell Daisy, Dillon, and the captain. He would enjoy rubbing this in the captain's face. Thinking about doing that, he broke into a wide grin.

"It's big. And this is where I'm going to need your help."

Jameson snapped back to the conversation. "Okay. Lay it on me."

"He's The Rook, man. It's fucking Sinclair. He even wears a ring with the symbol. The son-of-a-bitch has been flaunting it in front of our faces this whole time!" The detective's voice rose in frustration.

He plopped back down in his chair.

*Holy fuck. Sinclair is The Rook?*

"Tell me you've got him in custody."

Alonso growled, "Not yet. But we will." He continued in a more even tone, "This will tie him to the murder and the drugs, but we need you to share what you have on the Redland case. Evidence and all. It's going to help us put Sinclair away for good."

"Of course. Let's take the bastard down." Jameson didn't have to think twice. He'd share anything that put Sinclair in a cell, especially now, knowing what he'd tried to do to Daisy.

"Thanks, man. I'll send a car over when you give me the thumbs up."

"10-4. And Alonso?"

"Yeah?"

"I owe you one—for the video." He smiled. Today was his lucky day, it seemed.

"Yeah, yeah. I'll add it to the tab." Alonso ribbed him good-naturedly, and he chuckled in response.

When he hung up the phone, he felt like a crushing weight had been lifted from his shoulders. This was the last week before her preliminary hearing, and he'd been running out of time.

He owed Alonso big for this. He couldn't wait to tell Daisy. She'd be at work now, but he'd start the ball rolling to get her charges dismissed, then deliver the good news as soon as she finished her shift.

Whistling to himself, Jameson got to work.

# CHAPTER 19

*Jameson*

Monday evening, Jameson's good mood continued to hold. He was smiling as he climbed the steps to Daisy's apartment. After getting the video from Alonso, he'd updated Dillon and the captain, drafted the supplemental report with the evidence, and sent it to the DA's office. They would share the information with Blair as Daisy's criminal defense attorney and likely dismiss the charges. If not, he was confident Blair could negotiate them to that point. The video was enough to cast doubt on whatever Emerson had cooked up as the "probable cause" argument for the search, and it took any chance of proving her guilty beyond all reasonable doubt off the table.

They'd finally turned a corner, and she would be able to put this behind her. He'd been antsy all afternoon because he was eager to tell her. The trial date had been weighing on her no matter how she'd tried to hide it. She would be so relieved and happy that hopefully, it'd help him smooth everything else over with her. He needed that to happen because he *needed* her.

As he reached her door, his phone rang. Fishing it out of his pocket, he frowned at the number on the screen. A knot formed in his stomach, telling him something wasn't right.

"Judge Emerson?" he answered.

"Sergeant Jameson?" The judge's voice sounded strained, and his senses went on high alert.

He and Emerson hadn't exactly parted on friendly terms. Speculating on what had made the man call him, he stepped back from Daisy's door.

"Yes. What's going on, judge?"

"I need your protection. I can . . . I have information," he paused before whispering, "on the man you're looking for—The Rook."

His mind raced as he said, "You have my attention."

If the judge was offering to turn over on Sinclair, it could provide another link in the chain that would lock the bastard up for good. He'd have to run it by the captain and get approval from the county, but this was more good news.

"Give me twenty-four hours to arrange it and we'll deal."

"No!" The judge's voice spiked. "I can't wait that long. He's cleaning up. Look, sergeant, I hav—"

The sound of a gun firing echoed over the line before it went dead, and Jameson raced to his police cruiser.

*Fuck, fuck, fuck!*

He grabbed the radio and called in the shots fired. Not knowing where the judge had phoned from, he sent a car to the courthouse and the judge's residence. He hoped they'd find Emerson alive, but the way the man had been cut off made him think otherwise.

*So much for that extra link in the chain.*

Growling in disgust, he was about to gun it out of there and head for the judge's home when movement at the back of Daisy's building caught his eye.

The quadplex butted up against a narrow alleyway that was rarely used, and with adrenaline heightening his senses, alarm bells started going off. He put the cruiser in park and took a better look.

What he saw made his blood run cold.

Daisy was being ushered away from the building by a man he didn't recognize. One, who wore a suit with black driving gloves and, hugged her way too close to his side.

For that alone, Jameson wanted to kill him.

It was hard to tell from this angle, but her posture hinted that she wasn't going willingly, and he would bet the perp was holding a weapon on her.

With no time to call for backup, he leaped from the cruiser, pulled his weapon from the holster, and approached from behind.

As he closed within ten feet of the man and Daisy, he called out, "Police. Don't move."

Of course, the fucker didn't listen. He swung around with Daisy, who nearly fell at the jerkiness of the movement, and Jameson got a glimpse of the handgun shoved into her side.

The sight had his heartbeat racing as fear for her safety tried to overwhelm him. He struggled but was able to push it aside and focus on getting her out of this situation.

With a cooler head, he assessed the perp. The gun he held on her had a fucking suppressor on it, and the look in his dark brown eyes made Jameson's whole body tense. There was no fear there, just cold calculation.

This wasn't going to be easy.

"You're going to want to back away now. Daisy here's coming with me."

The man kept the gun trained on her abdomen and didn't even flinch at his weapon, which he'd pointed at the fucker's heart.

"Drop your firearm, or I'll be forced to shoot." He took a step closer and cursed under his breath when the perp took a step back, pulling Daisy with him.

He hadn't expected the man to comply but needed to stall until he figured out a way to neutralize the threat.

"I believe that's my line, sergeant. Place yours on the ground, or I'll deal with the woman right here." He shoved the handgun into her side again, and she yelped.

The sound made his adrenaline spike, and he focused on her face. She didn't look scared, which surprised him. In fact, her eyes squinted in anger. She was holding her own, and it impressed the hell out of him. Especially when his fear had turned into a tight ball in his stomach.

She twitched her head at him, trying to tell him something, and that ball started bouncing around in his gut. Whatever she wanted to do would likely get her shot.

He tried to convey that it was a bad idea with his eyes.

"You're trying my patience, cop," the perp growled and gestured with the gun he'd been holding on Daisy. "Yours on the ground or I—"

With the gun away from her side, she sprang into action. She took a step backward out of the gun's aim and swung the arm next to the perp up and back, slapping her palm right into his groin. He doubled over in pain, and she broke free of his grip.

As soon as she'd moved, Jameson charged forward. But before he reached them, the gun went off, and he saw her fall.

The sound tore through him, unleashing the fear he'd been working hard to keep at bay. His heart stopped, and he froze.

*Please, don't let her be hit. Tell me it missed her. It had to . . . Daisy can't be shot.*

The perp straightened, and his training took over. He aimed his weapon at the man's leg and fired, dropping the fucker to the ground. He fell with a howl but didn't let go of the gun.

Jameson was set to fire again, this time with deadly intent when Daisy kicked the gun from the perp's hand. It went flying across the sidewalk.

He'd been so focused on the man that he hadn't seen her get up. Relief washed over him like nothing he'd ever felt before, but he didn't have time to analyze it.

Rushing forward, he forced the man into a prone position and secured him with handcuffs. Then he swept his hands over the perp's body and confiscated a knife that had been hidden in his jacket.

With the man neutralized, Jameson pulled out his phone and dialed the station.

After explaining the situation, he ended the call and left

the perp lying there, knowing he wouldn't be able to stand on his own with the gunshot wound to his leg.

That was fine with Jameson. As far as he was concerned, the fucker could lie there and writhe in pain until the ambulance arrived.

He was glaring down at the man, wishing he'd shot him in the other leg, too, when Daisy's soft hand on his arm pulled him from the red haze that clouded his vision.

"James?" Her hesitant voice broke through his anger and had the fear coursing through him again.

Unable to speak, he pulled her in front of him and ran his hands over her. When he didn't find any injuries, he expelled a huge breath and crushed her to him in a tight hug.

He never wanted to let her go. She'd been so brave but so stupid! And she'd scared the shit out of him.

"Dammit, Daisy. That was reckless! You could've gotten yourself killed!" He squeezed her tighter, his embrace comforting despite the harshness of his words.

When she pushed against his chest, he loosened his hold but didn't let go. She glared up at him, and he loved seeing the fire in her eyes, loved that they were still open and able to shoot sparks at him.

"What was I supposed to do? Let him shoot you and then me?"

"No, I had a plan." He hadn't, but she didn't need to know that.

"Well, so did I." She pushed against his chest again, and he let her go with a sigh.

Clearly, she was still pissed at him. They needed to talk,

but now wasn't exactly the best time.

He turned his attention back to the man on the ground, made sure he was staying put, then went to retrieve the handgun the perp had fired. Thankfully, the shot had been poorly aimed and hit the pavement—not Daisy.

The image of her falling to the ground was on repeat in his mind, and he shoved it away. He returned to her side and really looked at her. Her complexion was a little pale around the edges, and he worried she might fall apart on him. Normally, a person would be in shock right now.

To distract her, he asked, "How'd you know to do that?"

She pulled her gaze from the man on the ground and answered him, "I didn't grow up with brothers and live in Chicago without learning some form of self-defense."

The perp tried to flip over and screamed in pain. Watching her, he saw her face blanch.

She mumbled, "But . . . I'm going to need to sit down now."

He reached for her arm as she wavered and helped her sit on the sidewalk.

When he had her seated, he lowered her head between her knees and spoke quietly, "Just breathe, Daisy. You're safe now. He can't hurt you."

She lifted teary eyes to him. "He was going to kill me."

He didn't respond, but she must have read the confirmation in his eyes.

"Why?" She searched his face, her brow furrowed in confusion, and he opened his mouth to tell her everything—about Sinclair and the judge—when the sound of sirens cut him off.

He glanced toward the road as two cruisers and an ambulance sped to a halt in front of them.

Resigned that it would have to wait, he stood up and glanced down at her. "We'll talk, I promise. But I have to handle this first. Stay put, and let the paramedics check you out. Okay?"

When she nodded, her eyes filled with questions he wanted so badly to answer, an uncomfortable weight settled in his chest. He wanted to hold her and reassure her of everything, but he had to do his job.

Bending down, he pressed his lips to her forehead and caressed her cheek. "Stay strong, Daisy. This will all be over soon."

# CHAPTER 20

*Jameson*

An hour later, Jameson had the scene in front of Daisy's apartment wrapped up. The perp had been transported to Dale County General Hospital under police custody. He'd question the bastard tomorrow after he received the required medical attention.

Sometimes, being a police officer had a war raging inside Jameson. He'd like to have let the man bleed out on the sidewalk, but he knew whatever information the perp had could help put Sinclair away and get Daisy's name cleared. He was positive the two were connected, especially after what the judge had said.

He sighed, thinking of that missed opportunity. He'd gotten word back from the officers who had gone to check out Judge Emerson's house. The judge was dead from a gunshot wound to the back of the head. So, the man had been right; Sinclair was clearing house.

Even though they'd lost whatever the judge could've

revealed, having the man who tried to take Daisy was a good thing. If she hadn't knocked his gun away, Jameson would've killed him, and they'd have lost that bargaining chip, too.

*Where is Daisy?*

He'd lost track of her during the debrief. Glancing around the parking lot, he didn't see her.

"Daniels," he called to the closest officer. "Where'd the woman go?"

The tall young officer gestured at the building behind him. "Back to her apartment."

"Did you get her statement?" Jameson snapped, annoyed that she'd gotten out of his sight.

They needed to talk, and it was hard to do that if she wasn't here.

"Of course, Sarge. What's the matter?"

He scowled and shook his head. It was no use taking his frustration out on Daniels. Ignoring the officer, he raced up the steps to Daisy's apartment.

A sense of déjà vu hit him, but his mood was a lot less buoyant than it had been when he'd made the climb only an hour before.

Reaching her door, he knocked and waited. There was no answer. Undeterred, he tried again, louder this time. He heard footsteps inside, but the door didn't open.

"Daisy, it's me. We have to talk."

He heard the lock release, and then there she was, as beautiful as ever. Knowing that losing her had been a very real possibility, the sight of her was salve on an open wound. It eased the weight in his chest and made him feel like he was seeing her again for the first time.

She still wore her uniform, which told him she hadn't been back in the apartment long. It reminded him of their first kiss. His eyes fell on her legs, but they were bare of those sexy stockings. She'd already removed them.

*Pity.*

But he loved the feel of her skin there and knew how good those uncovered legs felt wrapped around him.

Remembering it, he blushed and brought his gaze back to her face. Her black hair was pulled back in its habitual ponytail, making her cheekbones shine. They made him want to kiss her, but when he looked at her lips, they were pressed in a firm line, and her eyes were far from friendly.

He smiled sheepishly. "Hi."

She didn't say anything but motioned for him to come in.

He stepped inside and waited as she shut the door behind him.

Then, she stood in front of it with her arms crossed and raised an eyebrow at him. "I gave them my statement. Did you need something else?"

He frowned at her blasé attitude, but he pressed on. "Yes, can we sit? I've got a lot to go over."

She stayed right where she was at the door. "Like what?" she challenged.

"I was coming to tell you when"—his jaw flexed as he forced the words out—"that bastard grabbed you." He took a deep breath and continued, "We did it. We found the evidence we need to prove you were framed."

Her eyes widened, and her arms fell to her sides.

"What?"

"Can we please sit?" He motioned towards the couch.

In a daze now, she nodded. When she sat, he followed and lowered himself right next to her. He would've reached for her hand, but she had them clenched at her chest.

"Are you sure? How?"

He told her about finding the camera at Derrick's apartment and how it implicated Sinclair.

"What kind of person does something like that?" She gave a slight shake of her head as if she could erase the image he'd just painted for her.

Sinclair wasn't just a snake in the grass like they'd originally thought. He was a venomous viper hiding in the shadows, poised to strike.

He tried to reassure her. "The kind who belongs behind bars. Trust me, we're going to put him there, Daisy."

At her nod, he informed her that he'd already relayed everything to Dillon, that Blair knew, and that the charges would likely get dismissed.

She closed her eyes. He understood it was a lot to process, so he gave her a minute and said, "You'll be a free woman."

He reached for her hand and cupped it in his palms. It made him smile when she didn't try to pull away, but it was short-lived as he relayed the rest of his news. "There's more."

Her shoulders stiffened at his words, and he hoped she could handle what else he had to tell her. "Judge Emerson is dead."

At that, she gasped. He hadn't thought her face could

get any paler, but it did.

He rubbed the back of her palm with his thumb and hurried on, "He was ready to provide us with information on The Rook. I think Sinclair found out and got rid of him before he could do that."

"What about the man who . . ."

"He's in custody. I'll question him tomorrow, but my gut tells me Sinclair's behind this, too."

She nodded woodenly, and when he looked into her eyes, they'd gone glassy.

Wanting to offer her comfort but knowing she wasn't ready for it, he told her, "I called Dillon. It's not safe for you to be alone right now. Not until we have Sinclair in a cell."

"Okay." She pulled her hand back and leaned away, causing him to frown. "Thank you for letting me know. I appreciate what you've done for me."

It felt like she was dismissing him, but he was far from finished with the conversation. The reports he still had to write tonight could wait.

"You're welcome, but Daisy." He reached for her again, but she moved further away. "Look, I want to apologize."

"Oh?" She wouldn't look at him. Instead, she picked at the hem of her uniform and sounded only mildly interested in what he had to say. Her standoffish behavior was starting to annoy him.

He understood she was still mad, but she could at least allow him to make it right, especially after what they'd been through.

"I talked to Dillon . . . about us." That got her full attention.

She looked at him with wary eyes. "And?"

"And I was an idiot. I'm sorry I thought I needed to stay away from you in the first place, and I'm sorry I got upset after we . . . because you'd . . . you know." He rubbed at his neck as he fumbled for the right words. This had gone a lot smoother in his head.

She was grinning at him now, but it was practically feral. "You're sorry you were an idiot?"

"Yes?" He wasn't sure what she wanted him to say, and her expression gave nothing away. He felt like he squared off against an opponent with tricks up their sleeve.

"Is that all?" She watched him closely, but he was at a loss.

"I don't know what you want me to say here, Daisy." He stood and faced her, pulling at his hair with his hands. "I'm trying to make things right between us. Don't you want that?"

She shrugged and looked away.

He started to panic. The thought that she didn't want him anymore left him desperate. His heart was in his throat. It couldn't be too late.

*Tell me it's not too late.*

He hovered over her, unsure what to do. Not wanting to drive her away again, he waited.

Finally, she met his gaze. "Why?"

"Why what?"

*What am I missing? What is it she wants from me?*

"Why do you want to make things right between us?" Her eyes issued a challenge, and he blurted out the first thing that came to him.

"Because I love you, dammit!" His face blanched, and he dropped back to the couch.

*Son-of-a-bitch.*

He loved her. He loved Daisy. He'd said it in a moment of frustration, but it was true. He'd fallen for her. He was in love with his best friend's sister. And it was okay.

He wasn't sure if he'd needed the threat of losing her to realize it, but he knew now. She was the missing piece to the puzzle of his heart, and he couldn't let her go—not again.

* * * *

*Daisy*

Jameson's words had knocked the wind out of her, and she'd forgotten how to breathe. Daisy gasped for air, and he turned to look at her.

"I love you, Daisy." When he grabbed her hands this time, she didn't pull away.

She stared down at their clasped fingers and tried to process what he'd just told her.

*He loves me?*

A tingling spread through her, the current of electricity she always felt at his touch. It started in her hands and made its way to her chest, shocking the shards of her heart back to life.

"Daisy?" He whispered her name, and she met his gaze. His eyes held so many questions.

*Did she love him? Could she forgive him?*

She knew she still loved him, but could she forgive him?

She wasn't sure.

Her thoughts were scrambling to reconcile the way he'd treated her with what he'd said. Why did he push her away if he felt that way about her? Treat her like she meant nothing?

Her eyes filled with tears, and she tried and failed to blink them all back. As one leaked down her cheek, he released her hands to wipe it away.

"Talk to me," he coaxed, his voice low and gentle.

"You"—her voice trembled, so she took a deep breath and tried again—"You hurt me." She raised her chin in a dare for him to deny it.

If he truly loved her, she would forgive him, but it wouldn't be easy. Not after what he'd put her through.

He stroked her chin with his thumb, causing blood to rush through her veins and heat her skin. Her eyes fell to his lips. They were so close.

She shook herself. *Not yet!*

"I'm sorry I hurt you. Is that what I should've said?" He trailed a finger across her lips, and she held back a moan. "It's true." His eyes were sincere as they held hers. "I'm sorry for hurting you. Give me a chance to make up for it?"

He'd whispered the last sentence against her lips, and unbiddenly, they parted for him. She swallowed and closed her eyes, trying to block out the images of the two of them—skin to skin, his body sinking into hers on the couch—which flooded her brain and had her temperature rising.

She had a point to make, didn't she? With Jameson invading her senses, she wasn't sure why it was so important.

He caressed her cheek and cupped her face in his hands. "Do you love me?"

She opened her eyes and melted into his light blue ones. Overcome with emotion, she nodded in answer. She did love him. She'd never stopped.

He grinned and demanded, "Say it."

She laughed at that, enjoying the familiarity of the moment and hoping it would lead to the same thing. "I love you."

He smiled and lowered his lips to hers. It was gentle— the softest of pressures. The caress had warmth blooming in her chest, and she felt the pieces of her heart fuse back together.

When he ended the kiss, he pressed his forehead to hers. "I wish I could stay."

She leaned back, and he brushed a stray strand of hair behind her ear. "Why can't you?"

He sighed. "I have to go into the station and—"

His cellphone ringing cut off what he'd been about to say. He glanced at it and stood. "It's Dillon."

She nodded as he answered the call. Her thoughts were still racing after everything that had happened that day. She knew the man who had tried to hurt her couldn't get to her now, but she would feel safer with Jameson by her side. Not only that, but she wanted him in her bed. He had more groveling to do.

She was grinning at the thought when he ended the call with her brother.

"What is it?" He smiled back at her.

She shook her head. "What did Dillon have to say?"

"That I could finish my report in the morning." His eyes sparkled at her. "One of the perks of having your superior officer as your best friend." He winked and reached for her, lifting her off the couch. "And . . . he ordered me to stay here"—Jameson slowly drew her in close—"to protect you."

Daisy arched a brow as she stared up at him. "I thought I was the one that protected you."

He leaned down and nipped at her lip. "Fine. We'll protect each other."

She wrapped her arms around his neck. "Deal."

Grinning down at her, he asked, "So, Redland. What now?"

Her smile started small and grew until it was near bursting. "You mentioned something about making it up to me."

His eyes gleamed. "I did."

She dropped her arms and stepped back. Reaching for his hand, she entwined her fingers with his. They fit together perfectly. If hearts could smile, hers would be because she felt complete with their hands joined together.

On a high that can only be found with love, Daisy led him to her bedroom. They had almost two years to make up for, and she wanted to get started.

# EPILOGUE

## *2 Weeks Later*

*Daisy*

Daisy grinned as she took in the scene in front of her. Her family and friends gathered at the diner to celebrate her charges being dismissed. Shug had closed down early just for her. She would rather have brushed it under the rug and moved on, but she'd been outnumbered. So here they all were, laughing and smiling as they congratulated her. As if she'd won the lottery instead of having to deal with something that wasn't her fault in the first place.

She shook off the sour mood and glanced at Mr. Delacourt as he took a sip of champagne. He made a face that had her bursting out laughing. It was like a child who had tried something they didn't like for the first time.

He shrugged at her. "Can't say I've had champagne in a long time. Prefer a lager myself."

She settled down and gave him a one-armed hug. The other was holding onto her own glass of champagne. "Thank you for supporting me through all this, Mr. D."

The old man blushed, and it was adorable. Her heart warmed, and she was glad to have him on her team. Over the last month, he'd helped deter patrons who got a little too mouthy about her predicament and always defended her.

"You're welcome."

She nudged him with her elbow and changed the subject to ease his discomfort at her show of affection. "So, will you still come in here when I take over?"

She'd finally gotten the nerve to talk to Shug about buying the diner, and the older woman had been ecstatic. It might not happen for another six months, but the important thing was that it would. Daisy was beyond relieved to be making progress on her dreams.

"Of course! Well, as long as I can still get one of those Reubens." He was only half-joking, and she chuckled.

"You'll still be able to get a Reuben. I know not to spoil a good thing." She winked at him, then excused herself when she noticed her family waving for her attention.

Dillon, Lydia, Jake, and Blair were all discussing her case. She glanced past them and saw her mom and dad talking to Shug. Everyone she loved was here. Everyone but Jameson.

When she reached her brothers, the first thing they asked was, "Where's James?"

She smiled, perhaps a little too brightly. "He said he had to take care of something but that he'd make it as soon as he could."

In truth, she was a little disappointed that he wasn't here. The last two weeks with him had been wonderful, and she felt like they were finally past the hurdles that had kept them apart for so long. But for him not to be here . . . it stung a little. She was trying not to let it stir up past hurts and trust that he would make it.

Jake was grinning when he said, "I'm sure he'll be here any second."

She nodded in agreement. Her back was to the door when Jameson shoved it open. The blast of cold air hit her first. The temperature had dropped back down in the thirties. She shivered and turned around.

His arms were full with the largest sheet cake she'd ever seen. "All right, ladies and gentlemen, let's get this party started."

She smiled and felt like her face was glowing.

*He made it!*

Jameson returned her smile, and her heart turned over in her chest. She loved this man so much. They stood there smiling at each other like idiots until Jake and Dillon broke the moment by grabbing the cake. They took it from Jameson's arms and placed it on the counter.

He closed the distance between them and made her laugh by picking her up and swinging her around. But then she remembered the champagne. "Oh! Careful, it'll spill."

He took her glass and downed it in one go. "Problem solved." Then he picked her up and swung her again.

She laughed. Her head was spinning from the movement, the champagne, the giddy feeling she always got whenever he was around—or all three—she wasn't sure. "What's gotten into you?"

He placed her feet back on the ground and grinned. "We got Sinclair."

"We did?"

He nodded and brushed her hair behind her ear. "He's not getting off on a misunderstanding this time. With the added testimony from the perp that came after you, life in prison is the best he can hope for."

She stared into Jameson's eyes and felt free. The weight that had been dragging on her for weeks fell off as the end to the battle she'd been facing was finally within sight. "Good."

"There's something else." The way he stared at her made her pulse race. His eyes were overly bright, making her stomach jump with nerves.

*What else could there be?*

"Is it good news?"

"That depends." A grin flitted across his lips.

"On what?" She chewed the inside of her cheek as her mind filled with possibilities. None of them good.

"On you." He reached for her left hand, and the contact helped calm her.

She stared into his baby blues and searched for his meaning.

When he dropped to one knee, her mouth fell open. *Was he?*

He cleared his throat and tried to look serious, but his eyes still crinkled in the corners—the grin barely contained. He pulled a ring out of his pocket and offered it to her. It was a tear-shaped sapphire flanked by diamonds on a thin gold band. It was the most beautiful piece of jewelry she'd ever seen, and she instantly fell in love with it.

"Daisy Sarah Redland, I've wasted enough time already and don't want to waste anymore. Tell me you'll marry me."

She squeezed her eyes shut, but when she opened them, Jameson was still there, still waiting for her answer.

*Not a dream.*

She felt impossibly light as joy spread through her. It warmed her up from the inside so that it was as bright as a sunbeam when she smiled.

"Yes," she squeaked, her throat surprisingly dry.

His eyes were laughing at her. "Yes, what?"

She pulled him to his feet and cupped his face in her hands. "Yes, I'll marry you!" she shouted.

The room erupted with cheers as she pressed her lips to his.

When they separated, he slid the ring on her finger. Then he bussed her cheek and whispered in her ear, "You're mine."

His breath sent shivers racing toward her center. She grinned at him, her eyes wicked, as she whispered back, "And you're mine."

# A NOTE TO READERS

If you enjoyed this book, please consider leaving a review. They help spread the word about my books through the recommendation process and help new readers decide if they'll be a good fit for them. Reviews also contribute to my rankings on sites like Amazon, making my stories more visible to new readers. Even a one-line review makes a difference!

If you can't get enough of Rolling Brook, pick up the next book in the series, *Condemned by Secrets*. Remember Luther—the B&B owner's son who helped Jake when Blair went missing? This young cop gets his chance to be the hero when it comes to helping the new girl in town. Plus, there are some cameos you won't want to miss!

If you'd like a free novella set in the Rolling Brook world, subscribe to my newsletter. By signing up, you receive an EXCLUSIVE book featuring a woman on the run and forced proximity with a troubled military hero.

Want more updates, teasers, and giveaways? Follow me on social media.

All my links can be found here: https://linktr.ee/blyedonovan.

Thank you for reading!

xoxo,

Blye Donovan

# ACKNOWLEDGMENTS

I want to thank my fellow indie romance authors. This community is such a supportive one, and I am humbled to be a part of it.

My husband, whose support continues despite how many books I do or don't sell. Thank you for that and for being a sounding board and brainstorming partner for new ideas. And for allowing me access to your SME's (Thank you, J.T.!).

My critique partners. Ladies, your advice has been invaluable and has helped make this book so much better! Plus, I have to say a special thank you to M.K. for pointing out that my suspense novel needed more suspense. Your suggestion gave this book exactly what it required. I can't thank you enough for your help!

Lastly, thank you to all the readers who have fallen in love with the town of Rolling Brook and the Redland family. Your support keeps me sitting in front of the keyboard every day.

# BOOKS BY BLYE DONOVAN

**Rolling Brook Protectors**
*Hunted at Whiteford Farm*
*Gifts from a Stalker*
*Small Town Frame-up*
*Condemned by Secrets*
*Marked as Queen of Hearts*

**Stand-alone Novels**
*Undercover Santa*
*Blaze of Glory*

**Texas Heat Shared Series**
*Wait for You*

**TOP Security Series**
*Going Rogue*

# ABOUT THE AUTHOR

Blye Donovan is a military brat and a veteran who resides in the Lowcountry of South Carolina with her husband and fur-child, Maximus. Besides books, she's addicted to coffee, peanut butter, and shoes. When she's not feeding these addictions, she writes books  that are romantic suspense stories featuring strong heroines and alpha protector heroes overcoming dangerous villains. Her books are often set in small towns because she loves the atmosphere associated with them, especially when they have historic architecture. She was supposed to become a historic preservationist, but . . . writing has always been her passion. You can check out her current series, follow her on social media, and more all at this link: https://linktr.ee/blyedonovan.

9 798986 768328